Bidong

A novel
by Paul Phong Duong

Deux Voiliers Publishing

This is a work of fiction by an author with selective memory syndrome. Names, characters, places and incidents either are products of the author's imagination or are real events used fictitiously. Any resemblance to actual events or locales or persons, living or dead, is entirely coincidental.

Published by Deux Voiliers Publishing www.deuxvoiliers.com

Designed by Vu Nguyen

ISBN 978-0-9881048-2-2

Note - The historical citations on the history of Vietnam at the beginning of each chapter are taken from the Wikipedia article "History of Vietnam."

For my parents and siblings –
I will forever keep you in my heart.

The Dang Family –
Thank you.

For my family –
Lan, with much loves and respects.
Mi, you are the reason this book exists.

Acknowledgements

There are many people and organizations I would like to thank.

First and foremost, my wonderful wife, without her encouragement I wouldn't have written this book.

Gail William, Edward Sutton, Emillia Hunter, Michael Clementhall, John Phaphonsomkham, and Susan Sheppard, thank you for your input and keen eyes.

Laura Humeniuk and Ian Shaw of *Deux Voiliers Publishing*, whose remarkable copy-editing skills brought the book into its final form.

Vu Nguyen and John Nguyen, the best designers and friends I have ever known.

Vietnamese-Canadian Professional Association members, the best extended family a person could ever ask for.

Heather Pham from GIFTS Foundation, your work and dedication are inspiring.

And finally, Clayton Gomes, for being there when it counts.

A portion of the proceeds from sales of this book will be donated to help all the children of Heaven, the less fortunate people of Vietnam.

Prologue

Located about ten miles northeast of the small fishing village Merang, in the province of Kuala Terengganu, Malaysia, there is a small island called Bidong. About one square mile in size, it consists of inlets and rock outcroppings that spread all around the island and is used by local fishermen as a place to stop and take refuge during their journeys at sea. Due to a lack of drinkable water, the island was considered virtually uninhabitable.

In August 1978, the Malaysian government and United Nations High Commissioner for Refugees (UNHCR), in partnership with the Malaysian Red Crescent Society (MRCS), turned the island into a refugee camp. By June 1979, the island held more than 40,000 people, packed into an area the size of a football field. After more than ten years in operation, the camp officially closed on March 14, 1989.

Early Vietnamese refugees who fled their country found the island and lived there under trees and in makeshift tents, often having to trek miles up the mountain to find drinkable water. The living conditions were harsh. Many visitors who came to the island during the wave of the boat people referred to this place as Hell Isle. Families lived in one- or two- story makeshift huts built from the salvaged planks of destroyed boats, plastic sheets, cans, iron sheets, and cardboard boxes. Plumbing was non-existent, and when tropical storms hit, water would form filthy puddles around the living areas. Due to the location of the island, access was very difficult, and food and water was unimaginably scarce, to the point that it had to be rationed. There were many medical volunteers, but equipment and medicine were in very short supply. Sanitation became an issue and hepatitis spread wildly and quickly throughout the camp.

The mass of Vietnamese refugees became a major concern to the rest of the world. In July 1979, the Geneva Convention was invoked and the Vietnamese government agreed to curb the flow of refugees. Neighboring countries where many Vietnamese had fled agreed to take in all those who came, under the condition that western countries would guarantee that the refugees would eventually be assisted in settling in many of them. President Jimmy Carter took it upon himself to help with the resettlement process by increasing the quotas for immigrants entering into the United States. Countries like Canada followed his lead and significantly increased their immigration acceptance policies as well.

Bidong

Chapter 1

Hồng Bàng Dynasty (2879 – 258 BC)

The Hồng Bàng dynasty, also known as the Lạc Dynasty, is the first dynasty that ruled in Vietnam (then known as Văn Lang) from 2879 BC until 258 BC. Its founder is said to have been Hùng Vương.

Who am I? What am I?

The questions circle inside my head. Seemingly out of nowhere, the intercom interrupts my thoughts and the captain announces we will be landing shortly. *This is it*, I tell myself. This is the moment for which I've been waiting. My heart begins to pound and my blood pressure rapidly rises, causing me to stand. The flight attendant sees my uneasiness and approaches, requesting that I sit down and buckle up as we begin our descent into Tan Son Nhat airport.

I want to scream for the plane to hurry up and land. I'm anxious to kiss the ground. I want to bust open the emergency exit and parachute from the plane in the hope that it would be a quicker way to meet the land I have long forgotten.

Noticing my distress, my wife grabs and holds my hand. Warmth radiates through my body and soothes my agitated heart. I turn to look at her and see her pleading eyes. I sit down and settle in to look out the window.

Houses upon houses stagger over one another as far as the eye can see, competing with each other to be on the main road, the way trees in the forest lean over one another toward the sun. The crisscrossed roads are filled with cars, motorbikes, buses, and trucks following each other like ants marching toward their home. Smog hangs in the air from the millions of cars that navigate the tightly packed streets, and factories hum while thick smoke from their chimneys paints the sky gray.

Feeling suddenly claustrophobic and finding it hard to breathe just from the sight, I turn back to look at my wife.

"They used to call this Saigon," I say.

"They call it Ho Chi Minh City now," she adds, staring through the same window.

"It's so crowded."

"Yes. Eight million people occupy eight hundred square miles. It's one of the most densely populated cities in the world," she responds while checking out the hot, humid life below.

I am coming home. The thought races through my head like a flood, bringing with it many memories. Nostalgia and sorrow blend with bitterness and remorse. These memories that I have tried hard to file away deep in the ocean of my subconscious keep pushing to be released.

I sit staring at the lives of the many Vietnamese below, wondering how I came to be making this trip after so many years. Upon considering the notion initially, I had been filled first with hesitation and then with fear of the consequences it might bring. But my wife had insisted.

"At least see your birthplace," she had said. She kept telling me that knowing where I come from will help me to be a better person and a better father.

I asked her, "How will I be a better person just by seeing my birthplace?"

"If you don't know where you come, from how you can find out where you're going in life?" she had rationalized with a gentle smile on her face, the same smile that had stolen my heart.

"And," she had added, "don't you want to find out what happened to your family?"

I stare out the window again and lose myself in thoughts of my family and how much I have missed them. Will I recognize Mother and Sister? The thought of hugging Mother after so many years brings tears to my eyes. The feeling of being able to see my family after such a long time inflicts so much grief into my heart. Where are they now? Are they still alive? *Oh God, I hope they are.*

As if my wife hears the silent prayer, she squeezes my hands and gives me a comforting nod.

"Are you all right?" she asks. Without answering, I turn and look at my daughter sleeping sandwiched between us. She is but four years old, with a small dimple on her face every time she smiles and a strong resemblance of the mother I haven't seen since I was ten. Her face is so cute, with all her features seemingly placed carefully and gently upon it as though the Maker had dedicated more time to this little angel than anything else he had created.

Looking at her, I wonder. Would I have had the courage, like Mother, to put my faith in a puny little boat struggling across the ocean? Would I have let her become a refugee and settle in a strange land at such a tender age? Would I love her enough to sacrifice that love for her to let her follow her dream?

I don't know the answer to the question, but one thing is for certain; unlike that tragic trip that nearly cost my life, this time, holding my family's safety in my hands, I am taking no chances. I had gone to the library to research before leaving. A couple of weeks before embarking on the journey home, I studied Google maps with the hope of catching a glimpse of the little hut where I used to live. After many exhausting hours, I decided I had to see it again in person.

Together with my wife and daughter, venturing to Vietnam feels like the time Brother and I left this country: a journey of discovery. When we said goodbye to our country, we still had each other. Now, I return without him. What will I say to Mother about him? Will she be able to handle the news or will it kill her? I close my eyes and hope everything will turn out for the best. He was forty-two when he died. This trip would be much different if he were with us. He would have had the chance to see his wife and his beloved homeland. He had wanted so much to come home. He had worked so hard and given up so much, always in the hope of seeing our family all together again.

"Daddy, are we there yet?" Mai asks hesitantly.

"Soon." I look into her innocent face, so full of hope. "We are landing soon."

To move forward, I knew that I needed to know where I had come from. The thought lingers as I turn back to look out the window. Mai will finally get a chance to know where I came from. I hope she'll have a better understanding of herself, and won't live with regrets and confusion as I have for the past twenty years.

Unlike the reason I had for leaving home many years ago, the spark that set off this expedition started when Mai asked me a surprising question on the first day of school, when I stood outside waiting to pick her up. She had seen her friends get picked up by their grandparents and walk home hand-in-hand, dancing happily on the sidewalk.

"Daddy, where is your mother?" Mai had asked me because since birth, she hadn't seen a single member of my family.

I looked at her and my heart sank to the pavement. I didn't know what to tell her. A flood of emotions started to pour out of me and I mustered all my energy and effort to hold it in.

"Grandma is back home," I had said, fighting the roller coaster of emotions and tears that threatened to overwhelm me.

"Where is home, Daddy?" she had asked in the most gentle and innocent voice, though in my head it felt like a thunderclap. I didn't know how to answer her. I didn't know how to help her to understand where she came from because I didn't know myself. I was lost in the question.

Later that night I shared with my wife what had happened. She encouraged me to seek out my family. I hesitated at first, but finally began to pursue the idea. I told my employer I would be away for a few weeks. Out of concern he asked, "Where are you going?" He was compassionate and authorized all of the vacation time I had accumulated for the past several years when I told him, "I am going home."

"Daddy, I want to look out the window too." Mai interrupts my thoughts, putting her hands on my arm.

"Sure," I reply, stretching my hands over the armrest to pull her onto my lap. We sit silently staring into our country. A country where I was born, where Father lay waiting, where ancestors at rest watching over a new generation. A generation like Mai's, wanting to discover its roots, its identity.

Chapter 2

Thục Dynasty (257 – 207 BC)

By the third century BC, another Viet group, the Âu Việt, emigrated from present-day southern China to the Red River delta and mixed with the indigenous Văn Lang population. In 258 BC, a new kingdom, Âu Lạc, emerged as the union of the Âu Việt and the Lạc Việt, with Thục Phán proclaiming himself King An Dương Vương.

Sitting in silence with Mai, pictures of long ago begin flashing through my mind. I begin to reminisce about the early days of my life, where it all began.

There is an origin for everything in life. Trees have roots, water has its source, and humans have ancestors. My beginning was in a village called Vinh Hanh, a small farming community about 155 miles south of Saigon.

The village where I grew up was located between two mountains which stood like two guardian Colossi watching over the children of Heaven. Surrounding the sleepy village were green rice fields that seemed to stretch to the ends of the earth. The smell of young rice plants marinated the air and traveled throughout the village, lifting the spirit and calming the soul. The people of the village were at one with the earth and the Heaven, blending their rhythms under a blue sky to create one song—a lullaby. Every day was spring, and life was a beautiful song.

Walking into the village on the dirt road the first landmark to be seen was the village temple, the center for all holiday celebrations. It was a large, mysterious-looking structure with a perplexing inscription that welcomed all the creatures of the world to enter. Two large, pallid lion statues with fangs and claws framed the doorway, ready to jump into action as they guarded the many gods inside. The temple was the place where we held our annual harvest festival with games and contests for the young men and women. It was a time when everyone could lose themselves in celebrating our ancestors' passing and thank Heaven for another year of crops.

Beyond the temple, houses snaked along the road. Their doors were never locked, and guests were always welcome. Opposite from the houses there was a river where the water flowed clear, fresh, and cool. During the hot summer months, one could hear children laughing and giggling as they played near the riverbank.

Passing through to the end of the village was my house. It was a small hut made of green bamboo pillars, about the size of a compact one-bedroom apartment. Support beams were married with fresh green coconut leaves to form the roof. During the monsoon season, the house often leaked and painted the walls in earthy colors from the greenery.

In front of the house there was a small plot of land that my sister Mai had turned into a vegetable garden. It provided our family with a constant supply of mint, cilantro, and Asian basil. Inside our doorless house was an old table made of bamboo planks nailed tightly together. On it, there were always two cups and a pot of tea. Circling the table were four chairs made of tree stumps, quickly constructed without comfort in mind.

Further into the house were two makeshift wooden beds that had seen better days and on them our ragged blankets and pillows neatly folded. Immediately beyond that was our kitchen with its clay stove, pots and pans hanging on the walls, and dishes neatly stacked. Our drinking water came from a big jar located behind the house, and every day my sister would go to the river across the road to fill it up.

Just beyond our dwelling was the family paddy. The size of three soccer fields, it had been in our family since the early days of our ancestors. For generations as far back as Father knew, our family had been farmers. My grandparents grew up working the land and died on it. Father took over this noble trade when he turned fourteen.

Growing up in a farmer's family helped me appreciate the labor and dedication of my parents. They woke up before dawn every day and toiled in the field until darkness engulfed the village. While Sister and I stayed behind, my parents labored in the scorching sun—transplanting, managing the weeds, and fertilizing and irrigating the fragile rice plants that provided for our basic needs.

The grueling process of rice farming started with leveling the field. In the old days it was done by a hitch being dragged on the ground by water buffalo, plowing back and forth to soften the soil. The field was then flooded, which was the most essential part of the growing process. Once the land was perfect in softness and rich in nutrients, the rice planting began by hand.

Wading through the knee-deep water with seeds in their left hands, Mother and Father took each plant-seed and carefully buried it just deep enough for the seed to latch on, but not too deep to kill it. Every single rice plant had to be placed with love and care as if it was a brittle and delicate golden egg.

My parents used to claim that rice was gold because of the sweat, labor and time it took to acquire it. Whenever I accidentally dropped any food onto the table during dinner, Mother would make sure I picked it up for fear that any lost food, would be forever gone from my little life.

Compared to Mother, Father was a giant. He was tall and deeply tanned with long gray hair in a neat pigtail that fell down his back. His limbs were long and his hands were big. Only his eyes were small compared to the rest of his body.

Early in life we learned to both respect and fear our Father. He was a man of a few words. He never spoke more than was needed, but whatever he said was law. He didn't need to raise his voice, his gaze communicated loudly and clearly the different choice we should have made. He held the highest authority in our household and had the power to veto any and all decisions that were made. Fortunately though, he rarely exercised such authority. He preferred to spend his free time quietly watching the rice grow and sipping tea.

Father could spend all day sitting and staring at the green field in peace and tranquility. He told us that whenever he looked at our paddy, it evoked memories of his Father whom he had only known for a short time. It reminded him of who he was.

Growing up, Father had lived in a very lonely home. He was the only child in his family. His Mother had died during his birth, and when his Father passed away at an early age it left Father, only fourteen, to fend for himself. He struggled to farm the land that had been thrust upon him by fate. He managed to build a little hut in the middle of the farm for easy access, and for four years was alone in the rice field.

Father met Mother during a mid-autumn harvest. When the farm became too much for him to handle he had sought help from the villagers, but nobody stepped forward. He could only afford to pay with rice as wages, but it appeared no one was hungry enough to take on his substandard offer.

And yet as God so often has a plan for all of his creations, one person did accept his offer. She was a petite young woman with whom Father fell in love and later married.

Mother was a beautiful woman, slender in stature, with a cute little nose and lips that complemented the rest of her features. Her luminous eyes and the smile that dimpled her right cheek made her look much younger than she was. Her teeth were brighter and whiter than those of any other women of her generation, perhaps because she never smoked or chewed tobacco like many women in the village. She made a point of brushing her teeth after each and every meal to keep them healthy and clean. She was very proud of this.

Father made fun of Mother's oral health care every time she insisted that he do the same. He told her people had white teeth because they ate away their children's inheritance. I knew this was not true when it came to Mother because she was the most loving and caring person in the world. She was known in the village for her generosity. Whenever someone stopped by our house begging for food, she would give half our daily meal to them. This left us a little less to eat but we were content nonetheless because we knew it had pleased our Mother.

Sadly, Mother's relationship with her parents had also been a short one. At eight, her parents had died during a bomb raid. Alone in a shattered home with no source of food, she had been starving, thirsty, and lonely. Her hunger forced her to the streets, begging for food, but because of the war, there was never enough to go around. When she was lucky, monks would give her leftovers. It was months before her aunt found her, barely alive, curled up in the cold empty house eating sweet potato roots.

She moved in with her aunt and her four cousins. Her aunt was barely able to feed her own family so Mother helped out by planting a small vegetable garden in the front of their small hut and selling the produce at the local market. Living with her aunt's poor yet affectionate family instilled in Mother a longing for a big family of her own. When she met and married Father, she had just turned seventeen.

Most nights at our dinner table, Mother led the conversation. She was the one who reminded my sister and me who we were by using the many Buddhist lectures she had heard from the village temple. She was the person who taught me to stand up for myself and to follow my dreams. She taught me the value of being a person who contributes to society instead of being a leech that sucks away at life. I learned the many lessons of being human in a world full of hope and sorrow. She ingrained in me the love and respect for my siblings.

My mother taught us to be a family, with the oldest children looking after the younger ones when Mother and Father were not around. As the youngest, I was taught to simply listen and obey. The most important value that Mother made sure we would remember was never to raise our hands and hit one another because, as she said, "The bond between siblings is stronger than blood, and we shouldn't destroy it by hurting each other."

In our home, Mother was a source of knowledge and inspiration. She loved to learn and she had dreamed of becoming a teacher. When she was small she had taught herself to read and write, and when she grew older, she would stay up all night finishing any and all books she could find. Armed with a lust for knowledge, Mother had insisted that each of her children would have a proper education, and she bestowed that passion onto me as I was growing up. With Father, I learned fear and respect, but with Mother I learned to love and to read.

A year after my parents' marriage, my brother Tan was born. It was October 1962, the year of the Tiger. With much joy and celebration, Father had taken Tan around the village, introducing his firstborn son to everyone he met. He organized a great celebration, spending the family savings on a gigantic pig to feed everyone in the village. Poor Mother stayed awake for two days cooking for the many guests.

Of all the children, Tan looked the most like Mother, with his right-cheek dimpled smile, white sparkling teeth, and long hanging ears. He was short but muscular, which complemented his temper. When he was in school, he never liked to do homework, especially math. He would have tantrums fifteen minutes into a problem; he couldn't sit still long enough. He would throw his textbook to the corner of the room, cursing and screaming in frustration over the difficulty he was having.

At first, Mother would discipline Tan by having him stand in the corner for hours. But as things progressed, Father had to resort to spanking him. Tan's anger became more uncontrollable every passing day. At one point his anger resulted in his expulsion from school when he fought with his teacher. That day, Dad gave him such a spanking that nearly killed him; he couldn't walk for two weeks. That was the last day Tan attended school. He had had enough. At the age of fourteen, his highest level of education was the eighth grade.

In spite of his flaws, my brother cared deeply for Sister and me. When the rich kids in the village started flying kites and we didn't have any money to buy a fancy plastic one, Tan found paper and stayed up all night making one for Sister. Knowing Mai's love for cooking (her cooking was awful at first), Tan agreed to become her test subject. With each new dish Sister came up with, Brother would be both the first to try it and the first to get sick. Mother begged Mai to stop but Brother insisted she keep trying, encouraging her to keep doing what she loved most.

Knowing that I loved to read, Brother would walk across town just to find a book I had asked for. He saved what little money he had to buy me an expensive, rare book—*Tintin in the Land of the Soviets*, the first adventure of my childhood hero. And when I ran out of writing paper in the middle of the night doing homework, Brother would without a word march straight to the local shopkeeper's house, bang on the door, and plead with him to sell him a few sheets.

I idolized my brother when I was young. I took great pleasure in walking with him on the street and seeing fear in other people's eyes. I looked up to him and was in awe of the respect that he commanded. In my mind, he was a man among men, and I felt safe in his presence.

When Tan got married, he moved in with his wife's family. Every time he came home, Mother would make fun of him. She called him Thunder-Boy and asked him which of the sisters he had brought home that day. He would laugh at the inside joke and hug Mother. I asked Mother about the joke one day and she told me that in the beginning, Brother had fallen in love with the older sister of his wife. They had been dating for a year and had made many promises to have a wedding the following year. He had brought the girl home to get approval from Father.

Then, as fate would have it, Brother turned eighteen and was forced to join the military for a year. When he returned and went to see his girlfriend, she had decided a year was too long and had gotten married and moved to Saigon. She left him the dozens of letters and gifts he had sent while he was away.

Distraught by the news, Tan began drinking. He began his drinking regimen in the morning when he woke up and ended it when he was too drunk to stand. Day in and day out while our parents were busy in the rice field, Tan was busy drinking his life away. At first my parents thought it would go away on its own, that he would come to his senses and get over his puppy love. But things worsened, and violence began to accompany his drinking.

Things really began to unravel when he attempted to burn down his ex-girlfriend's house after a day of excess drinking. That was the day he met Loan, his ex-girlfriend's sister. As quickly as he fell into drinking, he fell madly in love with Loan. He begged her to marry him that very same day. Brother came home singing and dancing to present his new wife to our surprised parents. The village nicknamed the wedding Thunder-wedding and Brother, Thunder-boy, because they came fast and without warning, just like thunder.

Possibly because she had always been the only child in her own family, Mother had always wanted a girl with whom she could share her thoughts. Father knew of her wish and they tried to have another child. They waited nine years for my sister. Mai came into our family on a beautiful May afternoon in 1971, the year of the Pig. Mother was very happy when she arrived. She told me that she had pawned her wedding endowment to get Mai the prettiest clothes. Mother told Dad every time she bought Mai a new set of clothes that Mai had to dress better than anyone else because as a woman, you had to look your best.

Mai was tall and had natural curly hair. She looked different from the rest of our family. Her eyes were hazel instead of brown; her eyelashes were long and thick. She was so different that my parents often joked that she was adopted, but Father knew this not to be true because she resembled his mother, based on the one photograph that remained of her.

Mai developed a great talent for cooking, after her first ill-fated attempts. She would find ways to tweak a well-deserved rice sweet, and Brother would stuff himself to the point that when he walked away his belly protruded likes a pregnant woman's. Mai loved preparing food so much that she even played house with the neighborhood kids and pretended to be their mother, making real meals for them. She cooked many exotic dishes. Mother often wondered how she came up with the recipes, combining flavors in ways that had surely never existed until Sister came up with them. One such specialty was mushrooms marinated with fish sauce satay, with fish in coconut juice, lemon, salt and pepper.

At times, Sister would be so lost in her cooking she would forget about everything else. On one occasion, we were cooking sweet jelly pudding with several neighborhood kids. I was left in charge of boiling the sticky rice while Mai went inside to gather some spices for our playmates' meal. I waited for nearly two hours, and the rice began to burn. On the encouragement of my friends, I picked up the pot so the rice wouldn't be ruined completely. This turned out to be extremely bad judgment on my part because the pot was scorching hot and I couldn't hold it. Screaming in pain, I dropped it, spilling the contents onto my leg.

The next thing I knew, I was on the bed with my left leg swollen like a grapefruit and Mai by my side, apologizing profusely. She said she had been so busy marinating sesame seeds that she had forgotten about the pot outside. When Mother learned of my injury, we were no longer allowed to cook with the neighborhood kids or to cook at all without supervision. Despite it being forbidden, though, Mai's passion lingered.

Prior to my arrival, my parents though that with two beautiful children and a rice field to provide food for the family, they believed that God had smiled on them. Although they were not rich, they had a full life, and they felt that Fortune was on their side.

That all changed on a rainy October morning in 1979, the year of the Goat, when Fortune turned their world upside-down. That was the day I entered this world, a tiny baby with a congenital heart defect. I spent most of my childhood lying helpless in bed because I tired so easily.

As I grew up, Mother had to carry me to the doctor in the next village every week for a check-up and medication. My skin was pale with a bluish tint. My lips and fingernails resembled those of a person who had been in the cold far too long. I breathed at such a rapid rate that Mother was exhausted just watching my chest move up and down. I couldn't walk very far and I didn't eat very much. Compared to the other children in the neighborhood, I was very small.

I envied the other children who were able to run and jump and play in the river, giggling all day while I endured long hours in bed. I watched them, wishing I could play even simple games like tag. I wanted to run and join them, laughing, in their games. Many afternoons while lying in bed, I wished for just one day when my sickness would disappear and give me the chance to play like a normal kid. I would have traded years of my life just for that day.

The only activity that my parents allowed me was to go to school, and even that took a lot of work. To cover the three quarters of a mile from my house to the school took me an hour instead of the fifteen minutes it took the other kids. I had to take a break every five minutes and often by the time I finally reached the school, fatigue had set in. I had to fight hard to muster even a small amount of energy to carry me through the day's lessons.

My best friend was Hang, a girl around my age who happened to live next door to me. She had long black hair, a bulging forehead, and a walk that resembled a boy in a hurry. Hang was the only girl in a family of five boys, and she was also the youngest in her family.

Growing up, Hang was treated just like her brothers and often worked long and hard in the rice field until an accident with a rice tractor took her right hand. From then on her parents forced her to stay in and look after their home.

Hang and I attended the same class. She helped with class notes on the many days I was away at the doctor. We helped each other through the rough patches of growing up and she defended me when kids in the class picked on us after school. One time, the biggest kid in class called us names and teased me for my sickness. I couldn't handle it and decided to fight with him. It must not have gone well because the only thing I remember is lying unconscious on the ground and Hang having to drag me home.

Hang was such a good friend in my life that we made a pact to always be there for each other. And we were. We spent many days together catching butterflies and singing in the rain.

In my own family, Tan was the one who understood me the best. In my exhausted state, he was often the voice of encouragement and a defender against the kids who picked on me. Every time he visited home, he brought candy and let me ride on his back. Together we visited our parents in the rice field. We swam across the river to catch frogs and snails.

When he learned of the fight I had with the big kid at school, Tan was furious. When he asked me about it, I kept my mouth shut, fearing he might hurt somebody. Unable to pry it out of me, he went to Hang and forced it out of her, then marched straight to the kid's house and gave him a beating. From then on I was no longer "the sick kid" in my school. I was free to do what I pleased without being picked on. I looked up to Tan and admired his toughness, his no-nonsense personality, and his fearsome anger. I wished I could be just like him.

I looked forward to Brother's visits every week, not just for protection, but also for the many books he brought, especially *The Adventures of Tintin*. I fell in love with Tintin and his trusty dog Snowy. On days when Hang wasn't around, I found myself traveling with Tintin to exotic locations like the Sahara desert, the jungles of the Congo, and even the moon. Books helped me travel to places where I would never be able to go, and helped to relieve the pain and suffering I experienced because of my physical limitations.

My love of reading eventually inspired me to dream of a life far beyond that of a rice farmer's boy.

Chapter 3

Triệu Dynasty (207 – 111 BC)

In 207 BC, Qin warlord Triệu Đà defeated King An Dương Vương by having his son Trọng Thủy act as a spy after marrying An Dương Vương's daughter. Triệu Đà annexed Âu Lạc into his domain located in present-day Guangdong, southern China, then proclaimed himself king of a new independent kingdom, Nam Việt.

Like most farmers, my family was not rich, but we had everything we needed. We had enough to eat, enough to keep us warm, a roof over our heads, and most importantly, we had each other.

We depended on one another through the many hardships of life. In the flood of 1986, for example, I was seven years old. That was the worst monsoon season I had ever seen. It rained day and night, week after week. The perpetually black sky was constantly filled with clouds and rain. It was cold and wet all day, every day. I thought the sky had fallen and the world was going to end. It had rained so hard that the dam ruptured and flooded the village. Water was everywhere. The only proof that the village even existed was the roofs of houses protruding from the water and the scattered belongings floating around them.

Luckily for us, our house was situated atop a small hill. The water only flooded our home up to our knees. Father with his quick thinking added a few beams under our bed to push it above the water level. The bed became the only dry spot in the house. Everything under it was covered in muddy floodwater.

Soon the bed became the family kitchen. Pots and pans and our clay stove became my bunkmates. At night, I could barely turn without kicking a kettle or a wok. To make matters worse, when Mai cooked the smoke from the wet firewood filled our house and we felt suffocated, unable to get fresh air because of the unrelenting downpour outside.

The rain destroyed our harvest. We had to start conserving as much rice as we could. We had so little that there was no breakfast or lunch during those months; there just one meal a day and that was dinner. We adopted a routine of cooking congee—rice porridge—to extend the amount of rice available for dinner. That year, I remember congee being on the menu for dinner every day.

Those were dark moments in our lives. I slept a lot because I felt hungry all the time. I told myself that if I were sleeping, I wouldn't know I was hungry. So I slept for hours on end, awake only when my parents came home. At that point we would all eat dinner together in the dark.

To make ends meet, Mother and Father began fishing. They went out in the wet and chilly rain in their makeshift banana-canoe and only returned when it was too dark to see. In the evening their lips were blue and they trembled uncontrollably in the cold, wet clothes they had worn since the rain began.

When we were lucky, my sister was able to sell all the fish they had caught at the local market. But with the profits from selling catfish the size of three fingers, we could still only afford to buy rice and fish-sauce. That was all we had to look forward to every time Mother came back smiling from a good day's catch, but we ate without complaint because we knew there were many people who weren't as fortunate as we were.

During those dreadful days, our parents were hit the hardest, but at the same time they provided me with so much strength and courage that nothing in the world could compare. They loved Sister and me so much that they often went to sleep hungry, letting us share the tiny bowl of porridge. Many times they would skip eating altogether to give Tan's family something to eat. They never complained about how tough life was; and they were always cheerful when I saw them at night. We barely had enough to eat and the future was dark, but they continued to light my path.

Growing up, whenever someone told me that love could never make one full, I looked at my parents and I had to disagree. I know that during those bleak times Mother and Father got through because they had each other. They comforted and motivated each other to get up when they felt defeated. They patted one another's back when a job was well done. We were poor, but I knew, deep down inside, we were rich with something that no money could ever buy: Love. As long as I was bathed in that kind of love, I could be proud of being poor. My parents showed me that love conquers all and that the love of a family is the greatest love of all.

With our parents away working so often, the bond between Mai and me grew stronger as we helped each other take care of our little house. At the same time, we were taking care of each other with our motivation and encouragement.

When my stomach growled and hunger came knocking, Mai would bring me drinks, or scavenge through our rice pot for a nibble of rice to diminish my hunger. Despite the paltry food we had, she often secretly gave me little bits of her portions—though not too much, because she knew I wouldn't eat it if I thought she didn't have enough. We were more than brother and sister. We were the best of friends who happened to share the same blood, and the connection was stronger than steel.

After the flood began, my entire life revolved around the bed. The only job I had was to stay in bed and keep watch over our belongings. If the water got too high, my duty was to alert Mai and we would move to higher ground. In the beginning I waded in the water to get around, helping my sister cook our meals and helping my parents gather our belongings. But Father forbade even that limited amount of activity when we heard that one of the village kids had drowned. From then on, the bed and I truly became inseparable. I took Mother's words to heart and spent my time weaving many fantastic stories.

I began story-telling session in the hope of making my own small contribution to our family. I told tales from the many books I had read and stories that I had heard. When I ran out, I made up new ones. Often those stories were very childish, but my parents and Sister motivated me to keep trying. They told me that failure is the root of all success and never to give up. And so, instead of lying on the bed sleeping, I became a creative writer to entertain the family. I challenged myself to finish a story every day to help out, giving them a few minutes to relax and forget about the hardship of our situation.

In the dim candlelight, after we finished our dinner, everyone would gather around me and listen to the adventures I had come up with that day, like the adventures Tintin had in a water world where he had to travel by submarine down a thousand feet to fight a giant octopus with tentacles that could crush a house. Tintin also had to out-swim a nasty shark that could chew through metal, outsmart the one-handed pirate who made a living by juggling, and finally, sneak into an underwater dungeon to free his long-lost beloved sibling.

When I told these stories, everyone stared at my lips and watched every movement I made. Sister sat still and followed every syllable of my tale, hanging on to each sound and echo like a magnet. When I finished the stories, Father often smiled, patted me on the head, and complimented my creativity, making me very proud. I became the family's only source of entertainment and everyone looked forward to hearing my new creations. Even though it seemed very insignificant, I was excited to contribute something of my own.

When the water finally receded, school returned to normal. I was the most excited person in our class to be back. Besides Hang, Kiet and Thinh were also among my friends and classmates. They were boys around my age, skinny and freckled from constantly being in the sun.

Kiet was the tallest boy in our class. His job was to babysit a herd of buffalo from the neighboring village. He had to take the buffalo to the river to bathe them, then to the grassy area for feeding before bringing them home at sundown. During school, he would park the herd right outside our classroom. They were so close that I could put my hand out and pat them. It was a messy arrangement for our teacher because of all the noise and smell that came with them.

I loved hanging out with Kiet. I especially liked riding the buffalo. I remember the first time he offered me a ride after school. I was so scared that I would be thrown off its back and trampled to death. I sat completely still on the buffalo until it reached my house. It was fun, but I paid for it dearly. My body couldn't handle buffalo riding like regular people can; my heart was too fragile, and it cost me a week in bed.

Kiet was good at what he did. He enjoyed his job and made the most of it by studying and reading all day long while riding on the back of the animals. Whenever I had enough energy, I would watch the buffalo with him. Kiet knew the animals and understood them completely. He knew when they needed feeding or a bath simply from the way they mooed. He was even able to tell when they were about to get sick

Kiet and I shared a passion for reading. We would swap books and sometimes share each other's creative stories. Kiet and I enjoyed sitting in the shade reading all day. It was the best of times.

Thinh, who was short and funny, was the opposite of Kiet. He had a similar job but instead of water buffalo he babysat a group of ducks. He had to take the ducks and feed them in the grassland every day. He was constantly running around chasing the birds and as a result, he couldn't sit still and twitched constantly. Our class was like a carnival, where a battle of the bands occurred between the ducks, the buffalo and our teacher, all fighting for our attention.

Of all the students, Thinh tended to be the center of attention and the joker of our class. His punch lines were often about his ducks. If we knew why a chicken crossed the road, he asked us if we knew why the duck crossed the road. "Just like the chicken", Thinh said, "to get to the other side—and to pee. And he would walk around our chairs with his legs apart, like a duck in search of a bush to relieve itself in. The class roared with laughter and from then on Thinh was "Pee-king Duck," named after his favorite animal.

Every day, I looked forward to school. I liked to learn. I was constantly reminded by my delicate heart that I would never be like Kiet, running with buffaloes, or like Pee-King Duck, swimming around in the river. All I had were books. My body didn't have to be involved, and it didn't need to be used extensively. With books I flew all over the world. One minute I could be rescuing a damsel in distress and the next I could be in a spaceship traveling across the universe and exploring space.

One night at dinner I shared my enthusiasm about writing with Father, telling him that I dreamed of becoming a journalist like Tintin. I wanted to write books for children like me who couldn't lose themselves in games like tag or hide and seek. I wanted to transport children who could not walk or run to a world where they could fly, dance and sprint in the Olympic games, giving them a dream and hope.

Father was delighted, and he rubbed my head and told me it was a good dream and that I should do whatever I could to pursue it. Upon listening to my ardent dream, Mother, however, was overcome with sadness and distress, like someone had taken a knife and stabbed her from the inside. After a few moments of silence, she declared that she had lost her appetite and walked out into the front garden. Father followed a few moments later.

Confused, I turned to Sister and asked her what was wrong. Did I say something that may have hurt Mother? Then it hit me. We were farmers. I realized that our house was poor and we could barely get by, and yet here I was dreaming of going to university and becoming a journalist.

"We just don't have that kind of money," Sister said. She had already had to quit school because we could no longer afford her tuition.

I felt so selfish for having been thinking only of myself and not my family. That night I lay in bed feeling badly for making my parents unhappy. *I am such a bad child, I thought. I should be grateful they didn't throw me away and leave me to die when I was born. I am an ungrateful bastard.* I sobbed myself to sleep, but in sleep I dreamed of traveling to a university full of students, attending classrooms with books stacked to the ceiling and happily reading them all day long.

When I woke up I was still sad, knowing that the dream would never be fulfilled. On the way to school I stopped by the temple and prayed to the ancestors for help to make my wish come true.

A few days later, Father called me to his side. He told me that he had bought a pair of small pigs for me to tend. This, he said, would help me with my school tuition. When the pigs got bigger and had many little piglets, I could sell them and that would help pay for my education. I was ecstatic and smiled like a flower blooming in the morning sun. I hugged Father and Mother and rushed to tell Hang the news. The pigs were the topic of discussion in our class that month. I learned how to feed them and tend to their every need.

The pale looking pig that slept all the time I named Ti and the female with the stripe that constantly wanted to eat was named Teo. Every morning before I woke the pigs squealed and grunted, making a fuss and demanding to be fed. I stumbled out of bed wearily and grabbed the feeding bucket and water for them. At noon when I arrived home from school, I did the same thing all over again.

The pigs were dirty animals. They slept, ate, and went to the bathroom in the same place. After tending to their needs, my energy was always depleted. I would crash for the afternoon, knowing that when the sun set, those chores would need to be done again. Sometimes they wanted me to scratch their backs or they wouldn't eat. Other times, I had to read to them or they would throw a tantrum. They were like spoiled children who knew I had to love and care for them. Looking after them was hard work, but they provided much inspiration for stories. One of those stories was called "Who Has the Best Life?" written as an assignment for my teacher.

In a faraway jungle, there was a tiger who didn't know who he was. He planned to declare himself king of the jungle, and met with all the animals in the world to prove to himself that he was right. When all the animals gathered, he stood up on a great big rock and asked all of his subjects, "Who else has a better life than I? I am strong, wise and certainly living the most luxurious life. I don't even have to work very hard to eat." Being cocky, the tiger went around looking for acceptance and affirmation that others believed in him. If he saw an animal that had a better life than his, he would hunt it down and kill it. All over the animal kingdom the actions of the tiger brought great unrest. One day, the tiger came upon a group of horses and questioned, "Who do you know that has a better life than I? I am the King. I am big and strong. I can easily get food, unlike many of you who have to run around looking for it." The horses felt intimidated but replied, "Yes, sir. You're right, but I heard there is an animal that may have a better life than you." The tiger, furious at the news, demanded , "Who?" The horses were afraid to name the animal, so they told the tiger to seek out the elephant, because he has the best memory, "he will surely remember," the horses said.

The tiger ran through his kingdom until he came upon a herd of elephants. The tiger demanded that the elephants tell him the animal that had a better life than he did. The elephant thought for a long while but again, not wanting to upset the tiger and fearing for his life, he told the tiger to see the monkey among the trees in the jungle, because the monkey had traveled far and wide and knew a lot more.

So the tiger set out on a quest. A few days into his journey deep in the jungle, he spotted a group of monkeys in the trees. He asked the monkey, "Who do you know that has a better life than I do? I am the king of the jungle. I hunt my food. I am strong. I am wise. I can do anything I want." The monkey thought for a while then said, "No. I have seen the animal that has a far better life than you." The tiger grew very upset. He wanted to know who it was and wanted to see this animal for himself. The monkey replied that the pig had the best life. The tiger immediately asked the location of the pig, for he wanted to witness this unnatural phenomenon.

After getting directions from the monkey, the tiger set out on a long journey to a village. Upon entering the village, the tiger saw a pig sleeping in his stall. The tiger woke the pig and told the pig all that he had learned, whereupon the pig, smiling cheerfully, answered that he was correct. The tiger was furious. How could a small and fat pig have a better life than the king of the jungle? He challenged the pig to show him. The pig agreed to the tiger's request. He asked the tiger to hide behind a bush and witness a demonstration.

With the tiger in position, the pig started screaming "Oink! Oink! Oink!" and jumping up and down. A man rushed out of the house with food in his hands and fed the pig. The pig gulped it down and smirked at the tiger, showing him the attention that he had commanded. When the pig finished his food, again he screamed "Oink! Oink! Oink!" The man rushed out of his house again with a bucket of water for the pig to drink. Then the man washed and bathed the pig. The tiger, hiding in the bush, was full of jealousy and anger over what he had just witnessed. The pig clearly didn't do anything. He just waited around in his stall and a slave tended to his every need.

The tiger flew into a rage, demanding that the pig leave his stall or face death. Fearing for his life, the pig ran off, leaving the tiger in his stall. Now the tiger was full of joy, believing that, at last, he could command all of creation. So he did what the pig had done and screamed "Oink! Oink! Oink!"

Unfortunately for the tiger, it sounded more like a roar. The farmer rushed to investigate, found a tiger in his pig stall and immediately shot it. The animal kingdom returned to normal without the tiger around asking to be king.

The teacher must have liked the story because he read it aloud to the class. When he finished, he asked what the moral was. Being simply creative and young, I hadn't written the story with any forethought of a moral so I simply said "If you ever need anything, scream like a pig." The teacher laughed hysterically with my classmates, and Thinh started squealing like a pig in the middle of the class. That same night, my family got a good laugh about the new value I had learned.

In spite of being a poor farming family, we were proud of the fact that as a family, we cared for each other passionately. Father was the pillar that supported the many branches. Mother was the roof that protected us from the elements. Brother was the protector of the house and Sister, the caretaker. But all that would change. Life is not always spring and endless summer, and one moment can change life forever.

Chapter 4

Han domination (111 BC – 39 AD)

In 111 BC, Han troops invaded Nam Việt and established new territories, dividing Vietnam into Giao Chỉ (now the Red River delta); Cửu Chân from modern-day Thanh Hoá to Hà Tĩnh; and Nhật Nam, from modern-day Quảng Bình toHuế.

Sometimes in life we can look back and recognize the precise moment when things changed forever. In my case, it happened on a Sunday in February, six months after the pig entered our house. My parents hadn't come home for dinner that night and so after waiting up late, Sister and I went to the field with the hope that they were just busy and had forgotten about dinner. In the pitch-dark field, with a dim candle guiding us, we called out to our parents. We trudged up and down the rice field frantically. No one answered except the crickets and the frogs.

We stood in the middle of the rice field screaming until our mouths dried and our throats began to hurt. Fear took over, and I began to whine to Sister. "Please, Sister, find him. Find him. I want him to come home for dinner. We *will* find him, right? Mother will be found, right?" I kept nagging her for answers, only stopping when I noticed tears forming in her eyes.

Without much hope, we decided to check with the neighbor. We learned that while I was at school and Sister was away, my parents had come home abruptly in the afternoon and borrowed some money from the neighbors for a trip to the hospital in the city. Father had looked very ill, the neighbor added.

In my ten-year-old head, the thought of my Father in the hospital was inconceivable. He was built like a giant. He was strong and sturdy, a beam in the middle of our house that held it together. “This can’t be. He can’t be sick. He is a very healthy man,” I kept telling myself.

Sister and I stayed up late into the night listening to the motorcycles that passed by, hoping one of them would be our parents. Unable to fall asleep, I asked Mai what would happen to our little family if something happened to Father. Mai turned her back to me and pretended to sleep, but I knew she was awake because I could hear her quietly sobbing.

Lying in the dark, I quietly prayed to the ancestors and asked them to look after parents until a lucid rain snuck into my dream. The sky was sunny and dry, but rain appeared out of nowhere. I ran and took shelter under a tree, but somehow it followed me. I ran into our house, but couldn’t escape. It persisted. Tired of running, I stood still and closed my eyes in the hopes that eventually it would go away. It never did. It rained through my skin, seeped into my body. The coolness ran down my cheeks and saltiness lingered on the tip of my tongue. The rain touched my heart and crawled into my soul. My heart ached for it to stop and my soul discovered tears for the first time, whittled away.

Father didn't come home until the next evening. He was so tired that Mother had to help him to his bed. There he lay, his limbs stretched across it like a giant in slumber. I stood by his side looking at his exhausted features, too frightened to speak.

Fearing I might not have much time left with Father, when my bedtime came I asked Mother for permission to sleep next to him. As if she knew her children could soon be fatherless, she agreed.

Father coughed throughout the night and in the morning I could see blood had stained his shirt. His stomach gradually swelled. At first it was the size of a cantaloupe, but by morning it had grown to the size of a full-term pregnant woman's stomach. I lay next to Father for the next few days. At nights when he couldn't sleep, he patted me on the head and said, "You will have to be the man of the house. Be strong and take good care of the family."

I tried to take a day off from school to be with him, but he woke me early and told me to prepare to go. I told him that I wanted to be with him—afraid that if he left my sight I might not see him again. I wanted to spend every last moment with him, to sit by his bedside and comfort him, but Father insisted that I go to school.

Before I stepped out of the door, Father rubbed my head and told me to study hard. Despite my fears, absolute discipline and respect for my parents' teachings had the upper hand, and I departed.

Hang was waiting outside. We walked to the village temple and prayed to the ancestors for Father's quick recovery. I confessed to our ancestors that our family would be destroyed if anything happened to him. We left the temple, but I pleaded with every step on my way to school for the Heavens to have sympathy on our family.

Over the course of the next few weeks, Father had his life sucked out of him. He grew thinner but his stomach got bigger. He could only manage a couple of spoonful of the soup Mother cooked with so much care. He couldn't sit up, and so he just lay there. I took to massaging him with the hope that it would somehow heal him.

The neighbors came with money to help out and Mother spent it at the herb doctor every day. She labored for hours in the kitchen, boiling the many roots and leaves that had been prescribed, hoping a miracle would come.

As the days went by, Mother's exhaustion set in. I could see it on her face. There were dark circles around her eyes, her cheeks were pulled into her face, and her crow's feet became more evident. She smiled infrequently and spoke even less.

Tan became a permanent figure in our house again. He had to be responsible for his own young family, but he was still around to help Father when he needed to go to the washroom.

Mother comforted Sister and me by telling us that Father would soon be better and our family would be back to normal. I knew it was not true. Every day Father became weaker and his belly grew to the point where it appeared it might explode at any moment.

One day early in the evening, when the sun had provided its last drop of light, Father seemed to have some energy in his body. He called Sister, along with Mother, and me to his side.

"This may be the last family meeting we have," Father said, taking the time to look at all of us as if engraving one last image in his mind.

"Don't say that, dear. Things will be all right," Mother protested.

The house went very quiet, as if we all understood what was about to happen. Formerly a big man with broad shoulders, bright eyes, and bushy eyebrows who commanded attention, had become little more than skin covering bones.

"Manh, being the youngest in the family you must listen to your Mother and your sister. I am sorry I cannot take you to the harvest festival this year like I normally would. I am sorry I won't be around to teach you right and wrong in life and that I won't see you grow up." His last words trailed off quietly.

With that, Father went to sleep forever. Heaven took him. I had only known him for ten short years. Shocked and scared, I cried, screamed, and called out to Father. I shook him to wake him up, but he just lay there. Mother grabbed me and tucked me under her arm, as if to protect me from the many more hardships I would have to endure.

"I am sorry, Son. I am sorry your father had to go away. I am sorry I couldn't help him to stay with you a while longer," she said in agony, squeezing Sister and me harder in her warm embrace.

Tan appeared in the doorway and immediately rushed over to hold the benevolent man in his arms.

I pleaded to Tan to wake Father up. I pulled his hands, certain that somehow, through his magic touch he might revive Father. Tan just stood there. Mother grabbed us all tightly and we huddled together and cried.

Father couldn't die. He was strong, he was invincible. "Father, wake up!" I yelled at him. "He has to wake up," I told Mother. "This is not happening. This is a horrible dream. I've got to find a way to get out." I stood up and ran outside still yelling and calling to Father until my heart began to ache and I lay down and fell asleep in the middle of our rice field.

The funeral was arranged for the very next day. A big coffin lay in the middle of our house with incense burning around it. Tan and I stood in front of the wooden casket, thanking those who came to pay their respects by lighting incense for Father, and to say goodbye. People came from all over the village. Day and night they poured in. Some I knew, some were new to me, but all had great things to say about Father. When no one was around, our family gathered together with Father and treasured those last moments with him.

For three days, I stood by my Father's side. I was afraid that if I left I wouldn't ever see him again. I stood there and fought to stay awake with every ounce and fiber of my energy. I was guarding the most important treasure in life—the person who had given me life, taught me, and loved me unconditionally.

Father was laid to rest in the village cemetery behind the temple, next to our grandparents. As a farewell tradition, each family member presented a parting gift or memento dedicated to his passing. Mother cut a lock of her hair and placed it in Father's hands, symbolizing that she would forever be his wife. Mai had a small bowl of sweets she had tirelessly labored over the night before, with the special coconut juice that Father liked so much. She placed it next to his arm, hoping he would remember the sweetest moments in the afterlife. Tan presented Dad with his favorite Lotus Green tea. I ran to the spot where Father and I had eaten lunch during harvest season, grabbed a handful of his beloved rice plants and placed them next to his heart, hoping with them he could find happiness.

The house was not the same without Father. It felt empty. Even though our house was small, Father's presence had occupied a significant part of it. His departure left a vast amount of space that could never be filled.

Mother and Mai tried to get back to their normal routines; Mother in the rice fields and Mai in her vegetable garden. For my sake, everyone put on a brave face to convince me that everything would be all right and that life would go on. But at night when the masks were off or couldn't be seen, I could hear Mother sobbing quietly in her bed. When that happened, I would sneak over to her and lie next to her. She would hold me tightly in her arms and in our dreams we both visited Heaven in search of Father.

The moment Father left us was like the foundation of our house suddenly crumbling away. The house couldn't function properly any more. With nothing to support it, the roof caved in and our family changed forever. The change was so deep that I would soon forget who I was.

Chapter 5

Trưng Sisters (40 – 43)

In 40 AD, the Trưng Sisters led a successful revolt against Han Governor Tô Định and recaptured 65 states (including modern Guangxi). Trưng Trắc became the Queen (Trưng Nữ Vương).

We approach the Visa Officer and hand him our passports. He takes them and skims through all three, pausing to look at me. He says something in Vietnamese very quickly and I try to understand what he's saying. He switches to English.

"What is your name?" he demands.

"Manny. But my Vietnamese name is Manh, Manh Tran," I answer. It sounds so foreign. A name I once used but haven't heard for more than twenty years. It feels like becoming re-acquainted with a long-lost friend.

"Who are they?" He points to Jenny and Mai.

"My wife and child," I reply, looking at Jenny. She waves at the officer with a grin on her face.

"What is the purpose of your trip?"

I stand there looking at the young man in the faded orange uniform holding our passports and consider my answer. I want to tell him I am coming home, that I have returned. Doesn't he see that I am a fellow Vietnamese? I belong here. I have come back to my own kind after twenty years abroad.

"I am on vacation. I am a visitor." I reply.

A tourist in my own country? What an oxymoron. Like being a guest in your own house. Am I a sightseer? Don't I see this country as home anymore? When Mother left me in the arms of faith twenty years ago to escape this country I called home, I came to see that day as the one whereby I gave up my identity as a citizen of Vietnam. I considered myself a traitor to my own kind by not living among my people.

The Visa Officer stamps December 18, 2011 into our passports and says something in Vietnamese that his co-worker finds amusing. He starts to laugh. I wonder for a brief moment what he is laughing about but decide not to pursue it. I say, "Thank you" instead and hurry to the luggage pick-up line.

The line is already long, and people are grabbing their belongings and rushing off to meet their loved ones waiting outside. The atmosphere is full of joy and excitement.

The luggage carousel moves along and new luggage is dropped off. I stand there and revel in the nostalgia of coming back to the land that I have long forgotten.

It reminds me of Bidong, the refugee camp I called home for more than four years, and of Luly and Buon, friends I treasured during the many dark nights there. I wonder where Luly is right now and how her life turned out after the experiences in the camp. Did she ever settle in America and become a social worker like she wanted to?

"You must be an American," a voice says from behind me.

"Canadian," I answer, turning around to see who the voice belongs to.

It's a Vietnamese man in his mid-thirties with round-rim glasses and short tidy hair, wearing a navy blue shirt and a lot of cologne. He smiles at me.

"I couldn't help but overhear what the Visa Officer said to you earlier. Please don't mind him."

"What did he say?" I ask with interest.

"He said that you are a root forgetter."

A root forgetter is one who has no recollection of his heritage. Is that what I am? Considering all the emotions I have buried, maybe he's right. After settling in Canada I embraced the Canadian ways and traditions like a kid in a candy store and left my heritage behind, just as I left my brother. I refer to myself as a Canadian, and sing that Canada is my home and native land. I picked up a Canadian name and way of life, never once bothering to look back to find out where I came from. I never considered it, really, until that fateful day when Mai asked me about my parents and our home.

We introduce ourselves. Nhan is a teacher at the Saigon University, on his way back from an exhausting twenty-hour flight to and from a seminar at the University of California. Before we go our separate ways he hands me his business card and asks me to give him a call if ever I need help.

"We'll be in touch," I say as we wave goodbye.

We collect our luggage and walk through the sliding door, Jenny and Mai trailing behind me. The heat hits and it's almost unbearable, like someone suddenly turned on an oven right in our faces. Noise surrounds us like a war zone, with screaming and yelling mingling with what sounds like millions of hands simultaneously hitting car horns. The smoke from car exhaust fills the street with dense smog. Unable to breathe, we try to find a taxi.

Overwhelmed by the hectic scene, I bump into someone. I look down and there stands a little boy about six years old who asks me to buy a pack of cigarettes. I shake my head no and then he offers me a pack of gum. “No,” I say aloud before I continue walking. All of a sudden, I notice a group of people following behind us. Some want us to buy food; others ask us to spare some money. We jump into the first available taxi. We close the door immediately and ask to be taken to the nearest hotel. The driver starts down the street and I sit back and take a good look at my country for the first time in more than twenty years.

Mai looks at me and asks, “Daddy, where are we?”

“We are in Vietnam.” I reply, stroking her hair.

“Vietnam? Where is that? What are we doing here?” Mai asks in a soft voice, and turns to rest on Jenny. Before I can answer, she closes her eyes and goes to sleep.

“We are coming home,” I answer quietly. “And these people are my people.” The taxi navigates the flood of people while I sit back and remember many years ago when Brother and I said goodbye to this country, a country we thought we would never see again.

Chapter 6

From Eastern Han to Liang domination (43 – 544)

Learning a lesson from the Trưng revolt, the Han and other successful Chinese dynasties took measures to eliminate the power of the Vietnamese nobles.

My world was pitch dark. I couldn't even see my hands in front of my face. It was incredibly cramped. Someone kept bumping into me, pushing and shoving at me. I tried to move away, but the other person and I were too tightly packed together. I wanted to stretch my arms and legs, but the space limited my movement from doing anything other than staying still. The room reeked of urine and feces. The hot, stuffy air made the smell even worse. I tried to squeeze my face into the weak stream of air coming from a small air hole in the far right corner, but my efforts were fruitless because people were already packed into the corner. I tried to make out the faces that surrounded me, but it was too dark. I called out to Tan, only to be told to hush.

A baby cried out and was quickly silenced, though I could still hear it whimpering through someone's hand. I tried to find a spot to lie down. The floor jerked me forward. I stepped on someone else's foot and I quickly apologized, but no one seemed to care. We were too miserable and too afraid of discovery to care about something as small as a stepped-on foot.

The floor moved like a pendulum, and the motion of rocking back and forth pushed me to the brink of illness. I couldn't handle it any more. I called out to Tan, "I am going to throw up." A plastic bag was quickly shoved into my face and Tan's voice quietly told me to take some medication. I did, and a rush of sleepiness quickly engulfed me. I wondered if I should fight to stay awake? But what for? Why fight the inevitable?

A vivid dream came to me. It was a sunny afternoon in spring. Birds were singing and there were children giggling by the river. It had been three months since Father had been reunited with our ancestors.

I was in bed reading another Tintin adventure when a stranger showed up at our house dressed in a green and khaki uniform with a gold star embedded on his cap. "Where is your Mother?" He spoke with a heavy northern accent, sounding so foreign that I initially thought that he was lost and looking for directions. It was only after a few minutes of confusing discourse and hand signs that I realized he was looking for Mother.

He said he was from the Cooperative Party and was here to ask Mother to join a great cause. The Party, following theories penned by the great thinker Karl Marx, had thoughtfully decided that for the social welfare of our society, our farm would now become the property of the community.

Mother was in shock and disbelief at the news. She refused to give anything to the invisible hand that wanted to take our land—land that had been in our family for generations. It was the only means by which farmers like us could live. Mother pleaded and begged, but in the end it was futile.

The men came back a few days later, threatening to take our family to jail for not following their wishes. For that reason we would be labeled enemies of The Party, and enemies were not worthy of participating in the new world order. The world was now run by one party, and no one would be above the party, including God.

Mother was forced to sign a declaration stating that a distant relative of ours (one of whom we had never heard) was once an enemy of the state. Because of that, we lost our right to own land. Additionally, our basic rights to attend school and hold a job were forbidden, not just for a year or for a decade, but forever.

In Mother's eyes, her life's work was gone. Her cheerfulness and her inner glow vanished. After Father had passed away she had kept our family together by maintaining our rice field, the treasure Father had left behind. But now with that one signature, she had let it slip away. Not by her choice, but it still had happened. After that, Mother died a little more slowly and painfully with each passing day.

I was awoken by the sunlight that shone through the open lid of the crowded storage compartment. The clean ocean air refreshed my lungs and I felt exhilarated by the sense of freedom.

"You are free to go onto the deck now. Danger has passed," a voice announced from above. With Tan's help, I was able to pull myself out of the fish-holding compartment.

The open sea greeted me with a spatter of saltwater across my face. I stood amazed at the vast, endless body of water, feeling like a speck of dust. The waves seemed as high as mountains and the wind felt as strong as a knife that could cut through rocks. It treated the boat like a leaf in a gigantic lake; toying with it and laughing with the sheer intoxication of its power, the power of life and death.

I scanned the deck of the boat. I hadn't had much time to look the day before as Brother and I had been hurriedly ushered aboard and into hiding. It was bustling now and there wasn't much room to move about. People were already hunkering down, claiming what little real estate was available. The youngest I saw was a child only a few months old who was held by a young woman. The oldest was a man in his late sixties who had a long snowy beard and a body that seemed too frail for travel. People were scattered all about. Some clung for their lives to ropes or handholds, praying aloud for safety. Others huddled together, crying in solidarity for the journey they were taking.

Brother took us to an empty spot in front of the captain's cabin. The sun was beaming down with enormous heat, bringing thirst and hunger. Tan took a piece of bread from our bag and handed it to me with a bottle of water. He warned me that we only had two small loaves of bread and one bottle of water, so we needed to save some for later. Even though I was hungry, I didn't have the stomach to eat much, and after a few bites I handed the rest to Tan. I asked him when we would be arriving at this America where Mother was sending us. He told me that the people who'd brought us aboard had told him it would take about two days.

We sat quietly staring into the horizon and thinking about the life we had left behind. The sun slowly submerged into the ocean, painting the water with an orange hue and lighting it with glittering gold. Cries and moans began to emerge as the sun set like a goodbye from a faraway place. The old man with the snowy beard started to sob. Many other eyes also became rimmed with tears, and all seemed engulfed in loneliness. For the life we had chosen would take us far away from everything we had known.

For generations, we had lived on our family's land with our ancestors. We had our loved ones and our memories. We had called this country our home, but now we were escaping from it. It felt like a betrayal to secretly leave the country that had raised us, loved us, and provided for us.

"Mother, Father, I am sorry I am not around to help you now during your old age," a young man said to the wind, hoping his message would be carried to his parents and keep them warm on their lonely nights. "I am such a bad child, I didn't even say goodbye to you. Oh Mother, I didn't have a chance to see you one last time. Please forgive me." The wind only howled in return, like a ghost answering the prayer in the night.

"Dad, I am sorry I won't be around to help you with the farm," another voice added.

"We have left our ancestors behind. We have abandoned them." The old man moaned loudly as if to reiterate the actions we had taken. This act would make us lose part of our souls because as refugees we had to leave behind all the things we held dear.

The night set in and the cold emerged. The winds wailed while waves beat against the boat. "I'm tired," I told Tan. He told me to lie down and rest my head on his thigh. "I miss home," I continued. It had been two days since we left, and every moment without our family felt like an eternity of loneliness.

"I miss them, too," said Tan, "and my wife."

"We will see them all again soon. Right, Brother?" I heard nothing from him, only waves and the wind. Unable to hold back, I softly dissolved into tears and cried until sleep took me.

As I fell asleep I had a sudden intense memory of the moment when Mother had said goodbye. She had waited until I was about to leave for school. She had a desperate look on her face, but she tried hard not to show it. In truth, I think she didn't want to frighten me. She told me I would be leaving to go to America with Brother, and we would go that very afternoon after I came home from school. I would wait in front of the house for a stranger on a motorcycle who would take us to a nearby boat. I barely had enough time to hug her.

"Will you be coming with us soon, Mother?" I asked.

"Someday we will be together in America," she had replied, in a voice that suggested she knew she would never see her children again.

Later that day, just before the motorcycle departed, Mother took a jade necklace that Father had given her and placed it around my neck. "This will keep you safe," she said. "Don't forget my teachings as you walk through life." The echoes of her voice traveled through the air as the motorcycle separated us. And that was the last time I had seen my beloved Mother.

I woke when a man stepped on my foot. The sun was well above the water again, and people had begun to move about actively and with joy, preparing to enter America. They began to eat, celebrating the thought that they were almost at the promised land. We envisioned a country where roads were paved with gold, where every house had a car and a dog, where food was abundant and life was full of wonderful songs.

The biggest source of cheer was from a round-bellied man named Toi, a man with a booming laugh and a gold tooth. He had been a colonel during the war. He told us that America was a magical world, one where we wouldn't have to work hard to enjoy a home with air-conditioning and an electric stove. He came around the boat shaking hands with everyone and told me not to worry—he was the unquestioned leader of this boat and with his experience in the army he would take care of us all. With all the excitement in the air and the loud assurance of Colonel Toi, everyone ate and drank merrily, cheered by the thought that at any moment now we would arrive.

The sun moved from east to west. A day had gone by without land in sight. Mr. Toi's excitement subsided with time. We returned to our earlier spots and prepared for the oncoming night. The boat kept moving slowly southward, cutting through the water with great effort. Like an old man who had traveled many years on the sea's surface, this was just another long journey it had to endure quietly without complaint.

The boat was eerily quiet on the third day, except when the baby cried due to thirst and hunger. Its mother tried as best as she could to nurture it, pleading for water from the other passengers to soothe her baby's thirst, but everyone ignored her. Unable to accept her child's fate, the young mother sobbed uncontrollably and helplessly, stroking her baby. Out of despair, the baby cried itself to sleep. No one spoke. No one asked how much longer we had to wait. It was as if we all understood but were too afraid to face the truth—that we might all perish.

The third and fourth days came and went.

By the fifth day, all food and water was gone. Our throats had dried and my mouth hurt from salivating. My stomach stopped complaining and my energy ceased to exist. I just lay there on the deck, wanting to go to sleep.

One young woman couldn't endure to see me suffer. She huddled beside me, put her warm, gentle hand on my face, and encouraged me to hang on. She was in her early twenties with long, silky black hair and bright eyes. I thanked her quietly, and she smiled in return. Tan asked the woman her name. "Hoa," she said.

Through her conversation with Tan, I learned that Hoa was traveling alone. She was from the village next to ours, and she was the oldest in a family of five children. Her parents had sent her to America with the hope that she could work and help her struggling family. Being the eldest sibling, she had many burdens placed upon her. In addition to helping her parents in the field all day, when she got home she had to cook and clean for her four brothers and sisters. When money was tight, she baked sweet potatoes and sold them to the school kids in order to have enough money to buy new clothes.

Growing up, Hoa wanted to be a singer. She loved the many songs by Lam Phuong, like *Thanh Pho Buon*, *Co Ua*, and *Thu Sau*. These were the songs that she felt painted her life. Their lyrics portrayed the love and the everyday life of a family whose members struggled even to feed themselves.

Wishing to take my mind off the current situation on the boat, I requested that Hoa sing. Her vocals were sweet, tender, and soft. Her voice lifted away some of the pain and brought us to a faraway place. For a brief moment, my thirst and hunger vanished and the nimble little boat in the middle of this vast ocean, with its gradually dying cargo, simply didn't exist.

On the fifth night the monsters arrived. With the loud pounding of our engine, we didn't hear them until it was too late. They were quiet and deceptive. We were startled awake by a loud shout and the bright beam of light they shone at us. They were large and dark with infuriated eyes and fire screeching from their mouths, and they smelled like rats, rotten eggs and death. There were five of them, four of whom carried machetes. The fifth, the darkest and foulest of them all, carried a handgun. They spoke in a foreign language but from their actions I knew they wanted to pillage, to rape, and to kill. They picked us up one-by-one, like we were toys. When a young man who was traveling with the snowy-bearded man resisted and fought back, they slit his throat. Lying on the deck, he bled to death.

The monsters rumbled and grunted with eyes that saw only a chance for destruction. They ransacked our belongings looking for gold and other treasure. When they finished searching they ordered us to stand in a line, shoulder to shoulder, across the deck. They took gold rings, necklaces, and anything else of value that we had on us, including Mr. Toi's gold tooth. He didn't put up a fight, for he knew his life would end if he did.

Brother, with his quick thinking, snatched my necklace and placed it under his foot. When one of the beasts came to check me out, the flashlight shone in my eyes and his breath gave me a chill as though I were in the presence of Satan. The monster picked up my arms and popped opens my mouth, grunting in dissatisfaction when he saw nothing of interest. He moved on to Hoa. He aimed the flashlight at her and stood there as though mesmerized by the young girl. The others gathered to leer and debated what to do, speaking in their strange language that I could not understand. Then the darkest fiend loudly growled, sending the group into a flurry of excitement. Together they burst out laughing in agreement. Without bothering to search Hoa, they picked her up and carried her to their boat.

She screamed and fought to get away. At the top of her lungs, Hoa begged for some deities to come to her aid. She pleaded to Buddha, she screamed for protection from God, appealing to some greater beings to take her away from these evils.

Unable to bear the cries, Tan ran toward Hoa, but one of the monsters quickly knocked him unconscious.

Hoa's screams made us shiver down to our bones. They stirred the ocean and frightened the fish, but neither Buddha nor God came to her rescue.

When Hoa's screams subsided, I could hear the fiends laughing in satisfaction. Moments later Hoa returned to our boat with her clothes tattered, blood running down between her legs, and her hair clumped together. The monsters stood in their boat and convulsed with laughter at their accomplishment, their animal urges satisfied. They burned incense and put it at the front of their hull as if to ask God for forgiveness, then pulled away, still laughing.

My brother went to Hoa and tried to help her sit down, but she just stood there like a lifeless shell. I looked at her, and in her eyes there was no sign of the beautiful girl who had comforted me earlier. In the blink of an eye, Hoa dove off the deck and into the water.

Screaming her name I rushed forward, but the ocean had taken her body to her ancestors. I looked down into the deep black ocean. The glimmering of the moon gave the surface of the water a silvery glow.

I sat back next to my brother trembling in fear. How could such vicious monsters exist in this world? It was so cruel, the darkness that had taken Hoa. It was almost unspeakably evil. It had taken the shape of a man, but it was no man, it was the devil of the sea that seeks to destroy anything that represents beauty. Its only reason for survival was to destroy the beauty of creation, the human soul. The picture of the Sea Devil kept appearing in my head, and in my helplessness I prayed to the ancestors for help and comfort.

We had now been seven days at sea. My mouth hurt, my tongue ached and my throat felt like it was on fire. I lay despairingly next to Tan, who appeared to be handling it a bit better. The engine kept ticking away, always propelling us in the same direction. I lost hope that we would eventually land anywhere. My lips cracked and bled. I hadn't relieved myself in two days. My skin was dry and stiff. I lay under the scorching sun and closed my eyes. Sleep came and went, but the Sea Devil appeared every time I awoke.

The atmosphere on the boat was daunting. People were lying around waiting for whatever was coming. The baby that had cried a few days ago didn't wake from its sleep. Its mother didn't wake either. She lay lifelessly wrapped around her child. My own consciousness came and went. Once when I opened my eyes, I saw a few people query the captain—a small man with a face that was darkened from being at sea so long—as to when we might arrive at our destination. He kept saying that he had been told to head south on his compass, and that was what he was doing. He told everyone he was sorry that he couldn't help much, but he was just like all of us when he boarded the boat before the departure.

The next afternoon my body began to feel numb. I was no longer able to feel any pain. I thought of dying. I mustered all the energy I had left in my little body and told my brother to take care of himself. Fearing for my life, Tan hugged me in his arms and asked me not to speak. He told me to hang on while he asked Mr. Toi to spare some water for me. I could see that Tan had managed to crawl over to him. "Go away!" Mr. Toi screamed, holding his bottle of water to his chest with both hands like a treasure. "Please," my brother insisted. "Spare the kid some water," someone else agreed. Brother knelt by Mr. Toi's side, begging him to spare my life.

Afraid that Brother might snatch his water from him, Mr. Toi moved a few feet away. Tan clambered toward him without any sign of dignity. Angry, frustrated and without saying a word, Mr. Toi kicked at Tan's mid-section. Tan fell, tumbling to the deck and holding his gut. I yelled for Mr. Toi to stop, but no sound came out of my mouth. I tried to push myself to my feet, but my chest ached and my weary heart couldn't handle the exertion. It simply gave up and I blacked out.

The next thing I knew, my brother was by my side. The blows bruised his face and blood was oozing from a wound. He held his gut and told me he was sorry for not being able to take care of me. I wanted to tell him it was not his fault and that I missed our home, especially Mother and Sister. I felt cold, and I was so very tired. I fell asleep.

I drifted off and saw a bright light in front of me. I stepped into it and saw Father by my side looking at me with a smile. The light was bright. I couldn't make out what was in front of me, but I had the urge to move forward. Slowly I advanced. The light provided much warmth and comfort. I felt the same warmth I had experienced when Father carried me to visit his rice field with the smell of raisins lingering in the air. I continued to walk toward this light and, with every step I took, I felt warmer and happier. Suddenly, a familiar voice came to me, calling my name. It was a voice I had heard often. It was my brother's voice, calling out to me as it had the many times when he came home for a visit. It was a voice of love from an older brother.

Chapter 7

Anterior Lý Dynasty (544 – 602)

In the period between the beginning of the Chinese Age of Fragmentation to the end of the Tang Dynasty, several revolts against Chinese rule took place, such as those of Lý Bôn and his general and heir Triệu Quang Phục; and those of Mai Thúc Loan and Phùng Hưng.

I woke to find myself lying on a white bed with white sheets in a room with white curtains. There was an intravenous needle in my arm. A heart monitor was on my chest and I was in a white hospital gown. "Where am I? This must be heaven," I thought. "Where's Tan?" The room was bright with walls made out of cotton sheets, and people were screaming and moaning across from me. I saw a boy around my age staring back at me from another bed. I tried to smile but it hurt to move my lips.

A curtain was pulled open and a young Vietnamese nurse with her hair tied in a pigtail walked in. She placed her hand on my head to check my temperature.

"Where is my brother?" I asked worried about what had become of Tan. I prayed quietly in the back of my mind that the ancestors had protected him.

"You arrived here two days ago. Your brother must be with the others in the recovery area," the nurse replied in a gentle voice.

"I have to see him," I said, forcing myself to get up.

The nurse thought otherwise and ordered me to lie back. "You are too weak to move," she insisted.

When the nurse finally left the room, I turned to the boy next to me and asked his name.

"Buon," he told me.

"How long have you been here?" I inquired.

He just stared at the ceiling and began to weep quietly. He called out to his mother and father.

I wondered what was wrong, but didn't want to cause him any more grief. I turned away from him and fell asleep a moment later. I was taken back to the day when Ti and Teo were sold to the butcher. I had happy memories of those pigs. I remembered telling Mother I wanted to keep them longer, but she insisted that we needed the money. Mother told me she was preparing for me to go to a faraway place and we needed money for the journey. I asked her where I was going and she quietly told me that Brother and I would be leaving for America a place where I would have a bright future and an opportunity to follow my dreams. I asked if she would be there. She frowned and I saw her eyes turn red. She nodded without speaking a word, as though she was afraid to say anything more for fear she would break down.

I woke the next morning listening to the waves splashing on the beach next to the sickbay. I missed Tan terribly and began to worry about his health. The same nurse from the day before came in and I begged to see my brother. After a few moments of pleading she helped me to my feet but I was too weak to move and collapsed into her arms. She gently guided me toward the exit. The muscles in my legs had been unused for so long they had forgotten how to operate. I shook and quivered like a newborn lamb.

The holding area had a bare dirt floor and a barricaded fence making it look more like a prison cell than a rest area. People lay like sardines packed into a tin can. Most were sleeping; a few just stared into space. Tan lay at the far end of the room with his leg bandaged. On seeing me tottering towards him, he rushed over and we grabbed each other in a warm embrace. He told me he was glad to see me alive and safe. He held me in his arms and I felt so much warmth. We bathed in each other's comfort for a long moment before he invited me to lie down next to him.

While we lay there, Tan recounted what had happened on the boat. A few hours into my sleep, he had tried to wake me. He had called to me, but I hadn't answered him. He had shaken me, but I hadn't even flinched. He was scared and hadn't known what to do, so he kept jerking my body.

Suddenly an island came into sight, like a light at the end of a tunnel. When we got close to the shore, he had picked up my motionless body and run to the people waiting on the beach. The water was up to his neck. He didn't know until he handed me to someone and then collapsed that the coral had slashed and wounded his leg. When he showed me his bandaged leg, it was red with bloodstains around it.

"Lucky you're alive. I wouldn't know how to tell Mother if anything ever happened to you," Tan confessed.

I smiled and told him I wouldn't die and that we had to see Mother again.

Brother cheerfully said the hardship was over now and he would protect me, like an older brother should. Nothing in the world could destroy that bond.

A few hour later representatives from the United Nations arrived. They welcomed us to Bidong and told us we were lucky because the island was officially closed to all refugees the day after we landed. They took the people from our boat into a processing center where they took our pictures, fingerprinted us and interviewed us. They asked about my home and background, including the reason I left. I told them about the visit from the Party, about our land and about how Mother had had to sell all our possessions so we could make this journey.

On leaving the center I was given a used t-shirt, a cup, a toothbrush, a red bucket for water and an identification card with a big stamp on it that said "STATELESS." This was the label that forever changed my life.

The guide led us away from the administration office towards our new living quarters and things began to change dramatically. The stench from the overflow of garbage assaulted my nose. Rows and rows of houses climbed the mountain with dirty laundry hanging out to dry in the open, like lines of flags waving in the wind. The streets were littered with waste, and children with nothing else to do had turned it into a play area. Syringes were scattered in every corner of the camp and kids turned them into missiles and fired them at each other in a game of tag.

The island was divided into six different zones from A to F, each separated from the next by a drainage ditch that fed into the ocean. The ditches acted as plumbing to carry waste. Unfortunately, many people simply dumped solid waste in them to the point that man-made mountains of stinking crap piled up everywhere. Kids played around in this raw sewage, throwing feces like snowballs. I fought the urge to vomit when I passed through each area. Luckily, there was a constant breeze of fresh air from the ocean that caused the odor to slowly dissipate, but you could never escape the sight.

The guide pointed out the local market that was set up every morning, and the post office where we would get our mail. Finally, he showed me the school, which I eagerly anticipated attending.

We stopped at an entrance near the end of the long row of communal housing in zone F. The house was plain and messy, with dirty clothes and garbage clutter the dirt floor. It was about 12 feet deep and 8 feet wide, covered in wooden planks and aluminum sheets for walls and a roof. Salty rain had eaten away at the sheets and turned them a dark brown. On the ground floor there were two beds, one on each side of the room. The walls were filled with pots and pans, red plastic cups and dirty clothing. Further into the house, there was a set of stairs to the second level where there was a loft and an extra sleeping area. A poorly constructed wooden balcony built for one made the ramshackle house even uglier.

Before he left, the representative introduced Brother and me to Mr. Thuan, the leader of the house. He was a tall, skinny man with a woman tattooed on his left shoulder. He greeted us cheerfully and asked us where we came from and how we had found our journey. Unable to get the Sea Devil out of my mind, I recounted the details of our voyage to Mr. Thuan. When I finished, Mr. Thuan was able to sympathize for my loss but he didn't want me to drown in sorrow. He cheered me up by showing us around the neighborhood. He told us about food and water rations, where to line up and what rules to follow around the house. He recommended that we conserve food and water as much as we could because strict rations had been imposed, and we might have to go without food for long periods of time.

When we returned to the house we were surprised to find Mr. Toi there grinning at us. He told us he would be our housemate. He smirked at me with his missing tooth, then came over and put his hand on my shoulder and said he was glad I made it here alive. He quickly added provocatively "Too bad for the little child and mother on board. They weren't so lucky." On hearing that, Brother became very uneasy. As if Mr. Thuan understood, he scuttled us away and showed us to our sleeping area for some rest.

My area was on the top level with neither a pillow nor a blanket. Unable to sleep, I lay with my face to the wall. To my surprise, I saw writing with names and years on the walls, as though someone was trying to tell me how long it would take to leave the island. There was a number next to every name, representing the number of years that a person was imprisoned before release. The number "5" appeared many times on the wall. I wondered as I lay there, would I have to stay here for five years before I could reach America? Five years to see Mother? I missed her. I yearned to hear her voice, to eat her home-cooked meals.

I was ten years old and without a mother or a father. Was I destined to be without them forever? As I slept that night, I dreamed of a place filled with endless paddies, a house made of bamboo trees, a sister that loved to cook, and a mother who loved me. It also had a rundown school, scorching sun, and got dirty with every monsoon season. It was a spot I called home.

Chapter 8

From Sui to Tang domination (602 – 905)

Early in the 10th century, as China became politically fragmented, successive lords from the **Khúc family**, followed by **Dương Đình Nghệ**, ruled Giao Châu autonomously under the Tang title of Tiết Độ Sứ, Virtuous Lord, but stopping short of proclaiming themselves kings.

The rain came in patches. It would stop for a few moments only to regain strength and continue for days on end. The constant beating against the aluminum roof felt like the warning of more rain to come. It did, however, provide much needed fresh water to support the lives of refugees like myself. It also washed away all the garbage, dirt and sickness.

The only thing the rain could not wash away was the longing for home, for a place where everyone knew your name and where you lived. A place where friends and relatives knew and cared for you, where when you were sick people stopped by to check on your progress and to help without your asking. A place where you felt you belonged.

The rain ceased eventually, but it continued in our hearts. People would huddle around on their beds, look into the sky, and lose themselves thinking of the faraway places from which they had escaped. Many droplets emerged on the cheeks of our housemates. We tried to weep it away, but it kept coming back. We tried harder by keeping busy, but the rain remained and triumphed.

After settling into our new house, Brother took me to the school at the end of our district that reached out onto the main beach. I was introduced to a small, mature, blond woman named Mrs. Winona. She sat me in a class with fifteen children all around my age, and I began the sixth grade. So eager to learn, I stared at Mrs. Winona throughout the class like a tiger stalking its prey, never once letting her out of my sight. She often looked back at me and smiled gently, acknowledging and understanding my desire and thirst for knowledge.

When the class was over that afternoon, I looked around and saw the boy I had met earlier in the hospital. I leaned over to say hello, but he stood up and left, not wanting anything to do with me.

"His name is Buon. He's like that. Forget him. He doesn't like to talk to anyone," said a girl's voice from behind me.

Startled, I turned around. There stood a girl with long black hair tied into pigtails with eyes that glimmered behind thick, black glasses. She had a pointy chin and wore a striped green and red t-shirt a few sizes too big. Her pants were old, ragged, and stitched up.

She smiled and cheerfully introduced herself. "Luly," she said.

I introduced myself and explained to Luly that I was new to the island. Without another word, she took my hand and led me to the next room, which was small but overflowing with books. They were stacked up to the ceiling, row upon row waiting to take me away to some magical place. They were eager to teach me the history of the world, and to share their many theories and secrets of the universe. I entered the room, a thirsty traveler in the middle of a desert approaching an oasis.

I grabbed one and opened it, but the words were foreign to me, so I immediately put it back. I saw Tintin and flipped through a few pages, but I couldn't make out any of it. Luly showed me a Vietnamese-English dictionary in the reference area, and so I sat there with a notebook and started to write down words and their meanings until late in the evening. I got home after dinner and by dim candlelight studied some more. I began a journey to learn English.

Mrs. Winona became an indispensable part of my education. She took her lessons very seriously, taking the time to listen, correct, and encourage me to speak properly.

Every day after class when other students rushed home I stayed behind, where Mrs. Winona walked with me and taught me the basics of writing English. We started with math and science and finished with English literature. Mrs. Winona taught me the love she had for the classics. Together we pored through Shakespeare, Dickens and Austen.

The best thing about Mrs. Winona was that she understood the life of a refugee. She made me focus on learning rather than being homesick, she gave me extra homework and assignments, and she challenged my mind on many different levels, acting as a guide to help shape my young imagination. We grew very close.

Mrs. Winona shared her life memories with me. She said I resembled her late husband, and that we shared the same determinations and dreams. Mr. and Mrs. Winona had met and married right after teacher's college in London, England. For twenty-five years, they tried unsuccessfully to have children. Mr. Winona had passed away from a heart attack two years earlier. Stricken by depression, Mrs. Winona volunteered with the Red Crescent Society. She ended up in Bidong and began helping children like me. She found that helping others eased her own pain and made her happy, as she was when her husband was alive. She thanked God for this direction because it provided so much meaning to her life.

For three months, life on the island was good. I had little to eat, but enough to live, and I was happy to be attending school. I was lucky enough to have met a teacher who served as a guiding light on my journey to reach my dream.

One day though, while sitting in class listening to Mrs. Winona go over English sentence structure, my heart suddenly began to ache. It was like a pinch at first, but got worse as minutes went by, until it became so painful I collapsed in my chair.

I woke up in a hospital bed. My brother was by the bedside pacing frantically and unable to calm down. He smiled on seeing me open my eyes. He told me not to get up and that soon I would have an operation. "The doctor will fix your heart and you will be all right," he said.

Sure enough, a nurse came in and took me to the operating room moments later. A team of doctors in hospital gowns looked at me and gently explained how the heart works. In a normal heart, blood circulates through the body by entering through the right atrium to the right ventricle, and exits through the pulmonary artery to the lungs, where it picks up oxygen and discharges the carbon dioxide. From the lungs, blood returns to the left atrium, travels to the left ventricle, and is pumped to the rest of the body through the aorta. My heart, however, wasn't normal. It was quite the opposite.

"Will this stop me becoming tired?" I asked the doctor. I could see a smile under his surgical mask.

"You will be able to run with the kids on the beach," the doctor replied.

I was ecstatic.

After the surgery, I felt so much different. With every breath, I felt rejuvenated and energetic. I could feel every part of my body was ready to spring out of me. I felt like running, but the doctor recommended that I stay and rest in the intensive care unit for couple of weeks.

During those times in the hospital, Brother was by my side every day helping me recuperate. He brought lunch and dinner, big portions compared to our rations. I was surprised and questioned how he got them. He told me he had found a job at the administrative office doing roof repair and they paid him with food, so he had plenty to eat. I ate like a hungry dog until Tan showed up a few days later with his arm in a sling, limping with a crutch: an accidental slip, he had fallen and broken his arm.

We received regular food portions, evenly divided, provided by the sickbay. We sat on my bed and ate dinner together like we did at home. Tan, however, insisted I eat more than he to speed up my recovery. I didn't want Brother to starve so I did the same in return. Back and forth on the hospital bed, we passed our food, painting the bed with rice. We stopped when a nurse came in and complained. We just looked at each other and smiled. With his gentle voice, my brother told me to eat more to build up energy to learn and become a successful journalist as I had always wanted. I thanked him for caring. He rubbed my head with his left hand just like Father used to do and said something I would never forget. "That's what a brother is for."

The second week after my surgery, Luly came around and brought me homework. I thanked her for it and complained to her how boring the place was and wished that she would come more often. From then on, she came every day after class with assignments and helped me with my homework. She and I read books to each other to pass the time. We would take turns reading and, if we didn't know a word, the other would use the dictionary to look up its definition. We would play word games to test one another's vocabulary. We had fun and encouraged each other to learn.

One day while we were reading *Aladdin and the Magic Lamp,* I turned to Luly and asked, "If you could make a wish, what it would be?"

She looked at me for a long time and then told me she would wish to be back at home with her family. Rain droplets began to rim her gentle eyes and fog her glasses. She quickly wiped them away, but they kept coming back. They trickled down from her eyes onto her cheeks and fell from her face.

Luly grew up in a run-down neighborhood of Saigon. She was the oldest sibling in a family of five. Being two years older than the next eldest boy, her main job was to babysit her brothers while her parents went to work. To help her family earn more money, she cultivated a small vegetable plot in front of their house for money. Every morning she woke up at the crack of dawn, watered the vegetables and harvested all she could to sell at the local market. She would travel with her siblings, each carrying an oversized bag full of produce. Other vendors bigger and older than they were would push them around and they would often be left to squat at the end of the road, away from the main market path. People would pass by looking at the young children huddled together with puppy eyes and buy a bundle of watercress or a handful of mint out of pity. When they couldn't sell all of their inventory, they had the leftovers for dinner. Their parents would know how well they did based on what they were having for dinner.

After spending the morning at the local market, the group would go fishing in the afternoon. They had the most fun by the river, coming up with games to entertain themselves. Luly's favorite thing to do was make little clay animals. She made all kinds of animals and she was good at it, to the point that her house was full of little dogs, cats and birds. In the evening, Luly would cook for her family and she would give the money they made that day to her mother for Têt, Vietnamese New Year.

Every Têt was the same. Luly would get a new set of clothes and she would pass her old clothing to the sibling next in line. The chain continued down to the last of them. While other people enjoyed the Têt holidays, her family would be busy making treats to sell at the market. Their family was barely getting by when her mother got pregnant again. The Têt money they made that year was given to Luly for her trip to America with her uncle.

Seeing Luly's tears, I felt it was my fault for asking her the question that brought back painful memories. I turned and looked into Luly's eyes. "I could be your genie," I said. Luly looked at me quizzically. "But the only magic I can perform is listening to your troubles," I continued, smiling at her and hoping she would cheer up. She did. The rain droplets lifted from her eyes and the smile returned to her face. From that day on I was Luly's genie and she became my "Master." We were inseparable.

I felt like a new person after my surgery. I could walk farther than before without any need to stop and catch my breath. Every day after I finished dinner, I walked barefoot down to the beach feeling weightless, exhilarated, liberated. I no longer had to be chained to the bed. I was free as a bird. My legs could take me anywhere I desired.

Master and I began to explore the various zones of the island. We visited the A and C zone beach which was actually forbidden because it was situated in a very windy and rocky area. We would hide behind the temples and churches to gather up the many sweets people left behind after their worship. The place we enjoyed most was the Catholic Church on the mountain next to the A beach, across from the administrative office. It was quiet and we could sit in the shade and look out over the ocean and down at the rows of aluminum houses. Father Moore from the church gave us cookies, and because of this we looked forward to going up the hill each day. Afterward, we would head to the library and continue our studies.

One afternoon, instead of going to the church, Master took me to a Buddhist temple, believing there would be even more cookies. We went late in the afternoon but couldn't find any food at all. Instead we found Buon, the boy from the hospital, sitting in the main hall, sobbing and alone. We approached to say hello, but upon seeing us he walked away—he still didn't want anything to do with me. I thought him odd. He never spoke a word in class, never smiled, and just lived like a lonely duck. Every time I looked at him I saw despair, a lost soul. I couldn't help myself, I wished to befriend him. We chased after Buon to the beach, where he had settled under a tree and was looking out at the waves beating against the beach. Quietly, I sat down beside him and asked him to be my friend. He nodded.

"You miss home?" I asked, staring into the blue horizon.

"No, I miss my family," Buon replied without looking at me. I could feel through the sound of his voice that he was trying very hard not to show weakness or cry.

"Where is your family? How come they didn't travel with you on this trip?" I asked as the image of my mother and sister came to me. "Where are your father and mother?"

"Hunger took them," Buon told me quietly. Thunder echoed and surrounded the three of us, wind gusts hurling sand and blinding our eyes.

"The pirates took my older sister and the waves swept my one-year-old brother away." Buon spoke to me in a somber voice. My heart ached, Master's heart withered and Buon's heart died.

A week later, Buon trusted Master and me enough to share more of his tragic ordeal. His family had lived in Nha Trang, a city about 280 miles north of Saigon. Being fishermen all their lives, their livelihood was a small fishing boat that Buon's father used to bring food to the table. After the fall of Saigon and for the future of the children, his father had furtively decided to use the small fishing boat to travel across the open sea in search of a refugee camp called Bidong. Four days into their journey, the gas ran out. The boat drifted helplessly, at the mercy of the current. The family huddled together, trying to conserve as much food and water as they could. The parents prayed to their ancestors to save the children. The boat had drifted for another three days in the hot burning sun with no land in sight. Eventually all their food and water was gone. The boat got kicked back and forward when storms gathered above them, but the rain never came to give them any drinking water.

His little brother was the first to be reunited with their ancestors. The boat carried along in the massive ocean for another five days until they saw another boat on the horizon. With no equipment to call for help, and no energy left to try, they waited, at the mercy of whatever may come. They hoped the boat would be their savior and they were joyful at the thought of being rescue, despite being thirsty and hungry, in limbo between life and death. His parents didn't care about themselves. All they wanted was for God to spare their two remaining children, Buon and his older sister Thu. When the boat reached them, they realized their prayers had failed. For far from being saviors, an archfiend in human form appeared in front of them. The Sea Devil ransacked the small boat taking whatever they desired, including Buon's older sister. She screamed with all the life she had left in her. Her screams echoed in the emptiness of the open sea. Only the waves heard them.

The boat glided on aimlessly. His mother was the next to go, dying of hunger and thirst or perhaps from sorrow. Buon lay next to his mother for comfort. His consciousness came and went, and he was unable to distinguish his many dreams from reality; dreams of warmth and comfort with his family appeared in front of him. He saw his parents and siblings gathered around the house having dinner, celebrating Têt.

Then he felt a warm liquid flow into his mouth, a liquid that brought much needed life into his body. At first, he thought it was still a dream in which he was drinking the nectar of life. It soothed his throat and lungs. He continued to drink until it was all gone. When he opened his eyes, he saw his father's hands. He had cut his own flesh to feed Buon, his son, his own blood. The blood did indeed save Buon's life because a day later a cook on a merchant vessel spotted the unfortunate boat and alerted the captain. When the crew arrived, Buon was the only one with any vital signs.

Hearing Buon's story and recounting my own horrors, Buon and I came up with a system to get rid of the monsters that haunted us every time we let our minds go free. We never thought such evils could ever exist in the world until we had witnessed them. It had changed our lives forever. We were no longer able to live in peace as the demons kept appearing in our minds.

We wrote down what had happened on paper, put it in a box, tied it to a rock and hurled the box that contained our nightmares out to the deep ocean floor. Our system worked so well that the darkness drifted slowly away from me and from Buon. He smiled more, looked forward to every new day and started focusing on his studies.

The three of us became best friends.

Every day, we went to the library after class and to the beach in the evening. When hunger was upon us, we hunted field rats to trade with the administrative office for instant noodles. When water became scarce we'd hike up the mountain to search for fresh water. Life was tough, but we made the best of it, since there was no choice but to live in these conditions that bred violence, with so many mouths to feed and so few resources.

Chapter 9

Autonomy (905 – 938)

In 938, Southern Han sent troops to conquer autonomous Giao Châu. Ngô Quyền, Dương Đình Nghệ's son-in-law, defeated the Southern Han fleet at the Battle of Bạch Đằng River (938). He then proclaimed himself King Ngô and effectively began the age of independence for Vietnam.

The harsh conditions on the island became clearer the longer I lived there, like a Black Mamba finally showing its fangs, ready to kill at a moment's notice. Between the hot and humid conditions and so many people packed into a tiny space with no privacy, life was tense and grim. The many mouths to feed had become such a burden to the system that rations had to be strictly policed.

Tuesday of every week was food ration day. Multiple lines formed early at the administrative office in the sizzling sun. Some were so hungry they fell unconscious before their turn came. Others were victims of heat stroke and exhaustion. Fighting, bloodshed, and even murder occurred in broad daylight, often while people were lined up waiting for food.

The weekly ration was a cup of rice, a fish and three packs of instant noodles for every person. Food became such a commodity that many would kill for it.

The camp became a place where the strong survived and the weak died. Ex-military men banded together and formed legions and alliances for protection. They ran a black market for stolen food and manufactured alcohol, for which my brother was a regular customer. They also ran protection racketeering. If you didn't belong to a military group, you would be pushed and shoved and your food stolen.

Fear was a constant for those without protection such as Brother and me. It plagued the island. We were living day-by-day hoping that conditions would improve. The Security was overwhelmed by problems and could do little to help with the situation.

Feeling a lot better after my surgery, I wanted to contribute and help out with our rations. On Tuesday I lined up for food. The lines were long and snaked around the administrative office a few times. The day was breezy and high winds blew sand in our faces and made it hard to breathe. Master, Buon, and I huddled together for shelter. It had been more than three hours and the line moved slowly. A booming voice came from behind me. I looked up and there was Mr. Toi, smiling at me, with his missing tooth.

"Have you been waiting long?" he asked.

"Only three hours," I told him.

He took a look and frowned at the number of people that were waiting. Accepting it, he walked toward the end to line up. A few minutes later, he returned, as if he had forgotten to mention something important. He told me Tan was urgently looking for me.

I left the line to find Tan. When I looked back, I could see that Mr. Toi had taken my place. On the way home, I saw Brother sitting and drinking with his friend. I asked him what the urgent news was, and was met with surprise. It was then that I realized Mr. Toi's scheme.

I returned to Mr. Toi to reclaim my spot in line. He pretended not to hear me, and just stood there. I yelled louder but he ignored me. Security heard the commotion and walked over.

"What is going on?" asked the man in uniform.

"He wanted to cut in," Mr. Toi answered, "with his buddies." He gestured at Master and Buon.

"You took my spot," I challenged him.

"I'm a Colonel. I don't do such things." Mr. Toi said, informing Security of his position on the totem pole.

The security officer frowned and told me, "Everyone starts at the end and waits their turn." He pulled me away, and as I squinted back I could see Mr. Toi's missing-tooth victory smile. I was furious but Buon and Master helped me stay focused and joined me at the end of the line.

Late into the evening, we were the last people to get rations—half a cup of rice and two packs of noodles. "This is going to be a hungry week," I told myself. I walked home defeated, crying and feeling betrayed. Tan saw my miserable state and called me over. I told him the story and, without a word, he got up and went straight to Mr. Toi. I trailed behind Tan, and I could smell the alcohol through the air.

Mr. Toi was sitting in his sleeping area having dinner. He stood up when Brother entered the room. "Why did you trick a child to take his place in line?" Tan roared.

Mr. Toi looked at Brother and came closer to face his accuser. From the side, Mr. Toi was about a foot taller and rounder than Tan. The atmosphere was tense. Mr. Toi looked down at Tan and then said something I would never forget. "Stupid peasant rice farmers like you shouldn't speak to men in uniform like that. I am a colonel. I am very dignified, and deserve much respect. I would never do this thing you have accused me of." Mr. Toi pointed his index finger at Tan. "During the war, if a farmer boy like you ever spoke to me like that I would have had him whipped." Mr. Toi's eyes bulged and he waved his hands to shoo us away.

Tan was getting angrier. I could see his eyes turn red and his fists tighten. Within a second, Brother jumped up and threw a punch in Mr. Toi's face knocking him against the wall. Mr. Toi struggled to get up, holding his left eye. He rose and rushed at Tan, throwing him to the ground. Without hesitation, I tackled and pushed Mr. Toi back to the wall with my hands. He picked me up and yelled at the top of his lungs "I am going to kill you!" before throwing me to the ground. I hit the wooden beam, my head pounding, stars circling above me. I tried to get up. I saw Tan run toward Mr. Toi and wrestle him to the ground, both trying to outmaneuver the other to gain control. Then Mr. Thuan appeared at the door with Security to break up the fight.

Mr. Toi told them that brother and I had tried to rob him of his dinner. I was shocked. I told my side of the story, but in the end Security knew the role Mr. Toi played among his men. They took Brother away to the jail and left me there to fend for myself.

I'd had enough. I walked down to the beach to cool off. Walking past the unescorted minor housing, Buon saw me and decided to tag along. We sat under the coconut tree listening to the music of the ocean beating against the rocks. To cheer me up, Buon told me that soon we would be in America, where life would be a lot better.

It felt very lonely while Brother was away. I went back to my routine of studying. I spent all day in the library, only going home to eat and sleep. I spread thin what little food that I had left. On the fourth day I went home knowing there was nothing left to eat, and drank a cup of water to try to ease my hunger before I went to bed.

The house was empty except for Mr. Toi. After our fight I tried to stay away from him. He slept on the left side of the house and I slept on the right, so we were about ten feet apart. My stomach growled. I tossed and turned, unable to go to sleep.

Mr. Toi asked if I was hungry. Without waiting for a reply, he took the instant noodles from his little cupboard and put them in front of him. It was dark and light from a street lamp shone through the plastic curtain. I could see his eyes beaming at me, like a wolf creeping up on its prey. They were the same eyes that I had seen during the night at the sea: demon eyes, cold and dark. I couldn't help myself. I crawled over and put out my hand to grab the noodles, but Mr. Toi immediately jerked them back before I could snatch them. He shook his head back and forth. In the dark, I could see he was smiling at me, like a carnivore toying with his meal. I could see the hole from his missing tooth.

Without saying a word, he stood up and unzipped his pants. He quietly told me that people work for their food and I should do the same. He would give me the noodles if I helped him out, pointing to his crotch. I was disgusted and decided to leave, but he grabbed me and yanked my hair. The pain was unbearable.

He threw me against a wall. I looked up and saw he was coming for me. "Your brother is not around to protect you anymore, little ant," he whispered. He pinned me down and covered my mouth with his left hand while using his knees to hold me in place. He took his right hand and peeled his pants off, then took my hands and forced them to his crotch. "Work it, or you won't eat," he ordered. His face was so close that I could smell his breath, which stunk like a rotten tomato that had been fermenting. I squirmed for help. I turned and twisted, trying to get loose, but he was just too big, like a boulder on top of a bug. I held my hand tight into a fist, unwilling to do what he commanded. I fought to get loose and screamed, but his grip covered my mouth shut. Out of desperation, I grabbed his balls and squeezed as hard as I could. Screaming like a pig that had just been neutered, he released his grip and holding his little manhood, he balled up in a fetal position. On hearing the screams people poured in. Mr. Thuan appeared at the door. I ran over and told him what had happened. Nothing more was needed to explain why a grown man was half naked, squirming in pain and holding his crotch. Security took him away.

When the crowd dispersed I tried to get back to sleep. Shaking from what just happened, I lay facing the wall and convulsed uncontrollably. I wanted to cry but tears were no longer there. Something had changed inside. A shield had gone up and I was no longer able to feel any pain. I felt so dirty that I ran to the beach to clean my hands with sand until it hurt. I swam out into the dark ocean until I was almost too tired to continue. I decided to backstroke to shore and returned to the house. In the sleeping area, I felt very hungry, so I grabbed the noodles that still sat in Mr. Toi's corner. I ate in silence.

A few days later, Brother came back. His head was shaved like a young monk's. He put his hand on my shoulder. "We are alone here," he said. "We have to take care of each other. No one will hurt you any more, little brother." He looked at me and smiled, reminding me of Mother.

When Brother finished telling me how much he cared for me, he took a cigarette out of his shirt pocket. He put one in between his lips and fished a lighter from his jeans. I was surprised by the change in him, having never seen him smoke before.

"Do you miss home, Brother?" I asked him.

"I do, a lot. But I try not to think about it. I don't want to think about what and where we will be. Or how long we have to stay here. I hate the uncertainty." He paused, taking a drag on his cigarette.

"If I knew this would be our life, I wouldn't have let you come, little Brother. My job is to protect you, and I am not doing a very good job."

"I hope our ancestors will guide us through this island," I said, hoping to comfort Tan.

"Our ancestors? Where were they when we needed them on the boat? Where were they when you almost died? I stopped praying to our ancestors long ago," Tan said angrily. He got up and left the house, likely going to get drunk because that was what he did when he wasn't busy.

Looking back now, I understand that while I lost myself in books, Brother lost himself in alcohol. This was the beginning of a journey, which would take us on our separate ways.

That night, I prayed to my ancestors and to Father, and asked him to look after Tan. He needed help with all the inner turmoil he had to face. I prayed to the ancestors to help speed up our application to America and to help Brother find peace and happiness there.

Chapter 10

Ngô, Đinh, & Prior Lê dynasties (939 – 1009)

Ngô Quyền's untimely death after a short reign resulted in a power struggle for the throne, the country's first major civil war, The upheavals of Twelve warlords (Loạn Thập Nhị Sứ Quân). The war lasted from 945 AD to 967 AD when the clan led by Đinh Bộ Lĩnh defeated the other warlords, unifying the country.

It started on November 1, 1955, and lasted until April 30, 1975. The Vietnam War cost approximately 67,000 American servicemen and 5.5 million Vietnamese their lives. In the end, who won? No one. In war there are only losers. So why did more than five million people die? What was the spark that caused so much pain and suffering? So many theories claim to answer the question, but one thing was for certain. The Vietnamese people would have to pay the ultimate price for peace.

It had been more than two years since I came to the island called Bidong and every day I thought of leaving. I listened intently to the news for any sign that the delegation from any country would come and take me away from this miserable place. *Anywhere is better than here,* I told myself. Tan, on the other hand was lost in his wine. He no longer cared for anything besides his bottle, which he hid in the corner of the house. Even though alcohol was forbidden in the camp, he found it from people who shared the same interest.

America was the first country that Brother and I applied for during our first year on the island. I was among the many lined up in the 40-degree heat, hungry and thirsty, to fill out the application forms and book an interview. I told Brother the night before that the American representative would be here, and I had taken the necessary steps for our meeting. With a breath that stunk of alcohol, he simply said, “Okay” and went off to sleep.

I couldn’t go to sleep that night. I kept on worrying about the interview. What should I say? How would I say it properly? I pleaded to the Heavens to help me get through this trial.

Unable to sleep, I rose before dawn and went to Master’s house. I dragged her to the beach to do a mock English interview. Master made fun of me for worrying too much. I told her I had to since Tan was no longer able to help us out. I used to look up to him, but now all he cared about was his magic liquid. Master smirked and told me that for a young genie without any real magic, I was too much of a grown-up.

After an hour of practice I went home and prepared for school. Again, I reminded Brother about the schedule. He was a little amused, but not very excited. He joked that soon we would no longer have to eat noodles. Instead we would have Big Macs, like the McDonald’s advertisement in *The Adventures of Tintin*.

I stayed at the library and practiced English with Master and Buon until thirty minutes before the interview. I ran home quickly to put on my best shirt, which was a used hand-me-down two sizes too big. I combed my hair and brushed my teeth. The thought of leaving this island and living among Americans excited me. I would go to school, I would work hard and I would become a person who contributed great things to society, just like my parents wanted.

I arrived at the office fifteen minutes early. I couldn't see Tan anywhere, so I sat under the shade of a coconut tree hoping he would turn up soon. Time is funny. When you want it to slow down, it seems to move faster than the speed of light and when you want it to go faster, it slows like a constipated turtle.

The clock at the government office struck three. A woman in her early thirties with bleached blond hair opened the door and announced our appointment. I took a quick glance around, hoping Tan had appeared, but there was still no sign of him.

The office was bare with a little window on the left and a small desk with papers and yellow manila folders. A man with thick glasses, a neatly trimmed mustache, and a belly so big I could have fit inside it introduced himself as Steven.

We shook hands and he asked me to sit down. Steven took a seat opposite me, maneuvering his large body into the small space. He opened a file with photos of Brother and me, took a few minutes to study the file and then asked where Tan was.

Suddenly, the door to his office swung open and Tan walked in. The odor of alcohol filled the office like a wine cellar. He was clearly drunk and unable to walk straight, but he managed to get to the seat next to me and sit down. Steven took a moment to compose his thoughts, tapped his belly and announced the beginning of our interview.

All of a sudden, Brother jumped up and loudly slurred something I could not understand. I reached over and patted him on the back to try and calm him down, but he pushed my hands off and vomited all over the desk and onto Steven's lap. Steven angrily stood up, his eyebrows cocked. He ordered me to take Brother away immediately. I wanted to ask Steven for another chance. I wanted to grab his hand and pleaded for a few minutes to clean up so we could prove to him that we were good people. But Steven left the room and slammed the door loudly. And that was the end of our interview.

Helping Tan limp back to our house, I felt his weight heavy on my shoulders. About halfway home he fell to the ground, but I managed to get him back up again. He started to mumble something, but I was too upset to pay attention.

In my head I cursed at him for being so inconsiderate. How could he not understand the importance of this interview? This was our chance to leave the island. We could settle down in America and began our new life and stop fighting like savages for food.

When we passed the beach, I sat Tan down and tried to catch my breath. I looked at him with his shaved head and red bloodshot eyes, and he seemed remorseful and apologetic. He took a small plastic bottle from his back pocket and took a sip.

"I am sorry, Brother," he said in his drunken tone.

In silence, I stared into the ocean. The anger inside me started to boil. It came up into my throat. I squeezed my fist and started to breathe faster. Then it took hold of me.

"How could you!" I screamed, "This was the most important day of our lives." My breath ran like a freight train. "And you got drunk!" He looked away, pretending he was not listening.

"I can't believe it. We were about to go to America, and you had to get drunk and blow our chances."

"Do you know about the Vietnam War? Do you know how many of our people died during the war?" Brother yelled at me in return. "And now you want to live in their country? And beg them to accept you?"

"I don't know and I don't care!" I bellowed back with tears running down my face. "I don't care who fought the war. Or who was right or wrong. All I care about now is leaving this hell hole."

"I don't want to go to another country. It could be worse than here. You go on. If you want to be an American so badly, you can go alone. You want to beg people to accept you into their country?" Tan said, his words stumbling through his drunken tongue. "I miss our family, Manh. I know this interview was very important to you. I didn't want to blow it, but I don't want to be American. I'm afraid that when we get there, we will not even see each other. Do you understand? I don't want to change. I hate change." Tan said this soberly, as if to ask for understanding and forgiveness.

"No, I don't understand, Brother," I shouted at him. "I don't understand how you can find anything in drinking." Anger raged through my veins and I knew I didn't want to continue a conversation with this drunk any longer. I started to get up.

"I don't need to go to no stinking America. I have everything I need here," Tan said, waving his magic potions in front of me. I ran down the beach until I was too exhausted to go on, at which point, I sat by the rocks and stared into the horizon, wondering what would become of my life.

When I woke the next day, Tan was sitting at the edge of the bed, smoking like he was lost in his thoughts. On seeing me get up, he turned to look at me. "Do you remember the time when we caught frogs in our paddy to have frog-congee and you accidentally fell into the neighbor's pond?"

"Yes," I replied. "I remember you jumped in and saved me."

"I thought you were going to die. Seeing you gasping for air, I had to jump in."

"When you got me out, somehow the fish had gotten into your shorts and you jumped around like a frog," I said smiling.

"Yes, I remember that. I made fish-congee instead and Mai liked it so much she finished the whole pot. She even commented that the fish tasted a bit different." Brother and I started to laugh. We woke the house up and people were curious about what was so funny.

"Brother, listen," Tan said seriously. "I didn't mean for things to turn out the way they did yesterday."

"I'm sorry I got so angry with you." I said.

"I have been very selfish. I have been drinking to ease my pain and I forgot about you. You are young and you have a future ahead of you. I haven't been a good brother to you." My brother said this quietly while I stared at my feet.

He got up and rubbed my head with his hand and said that when a new delegate came to the island, we would apply again. This time, he added, he would line up.

As I write this story, America is fighting in Iraq and Afghanistan. They announced to the world that they were successfully accomplishing what they set out to do—dismantle the weapons of mass destruction in Iraq and bring democracy to the Afghan people. I can't help but wonder who will pay for such victories? Will it be like the Vietnam War, where the Vietnamese people had to pay with the many deaths in the so-called re-education camps, so hungry that they had to eat that indigestible fruit called *bonbon* to quell their hunger? Because America is a fast food nation, they take your order and drive away, and never have the patience to finish what they have started. In the end there is no real winner when it comes to war, only collateral damage.

Tan had a point about not wanting to come to America. He was old enough to see the war first hand, and experience it as a citizen who loves peace. I, on the other hand, was too young and too ignorant to see how those events affected Tan throughout his life. Being young and full of hope, witnessing the horror of life in a refugee camp had had a major emotional effect on me. It was a trauma that caused us to drift apart and eventually destroyed our bond.

Chapter 11

Lý, Trần, & Hồ dynasties (1009 – 1407)

When the king Lê Long Đĩnh died in 1009 AD, a Palace Guard Commander named Lý Công Uẩn was nominated by the court to take over the throne, and founded the Lý dynasty.

Living on the island, every day became a struggle. The constant fight for food had become an expectation, and death was no stranger to the life of a traitor—a person who abandoned their country. Adding to the misery was the uncertainty over when we would leave. It was as though we had been sentenced for life. Dark clouds hung over our heads and anger rampaged through the camps. Bitterness for the hand we had been dealt led many to drown themselves in alcohol.

To bring some hope into our very chaotic lives, Master, Buon, and I began a ritual. Every Wednesday at noon we would gather in front of the post office and listen to the mail call. We hoped somehow we would be called to join the few lucky recipients of a Christmas present in July. We knew we would never receive anything, but we did it just to keep some hope alive, because hope was all we had. Without it we would have ended up like many of the other kids who threw their lives away on drugs or in gang warfare.

Out of the three of us, Master was the one who had been living in the refugee camp the longest. She had been there two years prior to Buon's and my arrival. Master and her uncle had applied to settle in America before but had been rejected due to a lack of proof of military service. Her uncle had served alongside the Americans during the Vietnam War, but when Saigon fell he burned and destroyed any evidence of his military past, fearing incrimination.

When the American delegate asked for proof of this claim during the interview, Master's uncle was able to recite his service number, his unit and the battalion to which he belonged. However, due to the lack of any physical evidence, the file was put on hold for further review.

Nonetheless, Master never gave up hope. Every few months or so she and her uncle would visit the administrative office and file an inquiry on the status of their application with the hope that someone in that faraway place called the United States of America would make the connection, verify the information and send her a lifeline. Waiting for that day had kept her working hard on her English and gave her reason to move forward with her life.

Master was my guiding light during those dark days following my rejection by the American delegate. Without her to push me forward, I might have followed Brother's example and drowned myself in poison. Or perhaps I would have jumped off a cliff or wrestled a shark—anything for a quick exit out of that miserable place called a refugee camp. It was more a place of torment than a camp. I was young and life was harsh, and I didn't want to live anymore. I was distraught, and would keep to myself most days. I often went to the beach and just stared out into the water. I would cry about missing home, cursing my situation. Out of concern, Master would come and drag me back to the library to study. She picked me up when I needed her most.

To keep the hope of a future alive and give us something to look forward to, Master came up with a plan. Sitting in the library, she asked me and Buon to write down what we imagined for ourselves, a career in the future. She wanted us to remind ourselves of this goal every day, to forget all the wretchedness that was happening in the camp.

Master began. She said that if she ever had the chance to go to school, she would like to be a social worker. She told me she wanted to help children without parents, like us, and guide them to walk the right path. This was a passion she could see herself following because she had experienced such a bad life herself.

When it was my turn, I shared with Master and Buon my desire to become a journalist. I loved to write and to read. I wished that someday I could help kids who couldn't walk enjoy reading my stories as much as I enjoyed writing them.

After I finished sharing my dream, I looked forward to hear Buon's. Master and I turned our attention to him. However, over the course of time since we began the writing exercise, he had changed somehow. He kept looking down at his feet like something had been triggered inside of him. When we asked what he wanted to do, he didn't bother to answer, just ignored us completely. Not wanting to agitate Buon, Master and I discussed presenting the idea to our class.

Mrs. Winona was elated upon hearing the idea. I became the class captain, holding and keeping each of my classmate's precious dreams. I would pass out dream paper every week before class began, and we dedicated an hour to writing, sometimes adding to our dreams and sometimes changing them completely. We shaped our futures instead of drowning in our sorrows. We imagined the jobs we were going to have, the food we were going to eat and the friends who would endure. We often came up with unbelievable stories, such as eating rice and fried fish in McDonald's or driving cars with wings. The whole class jumped on the bandwagon to see who could create the most ridiculous dream and those dreams kept our hopes alive, giving us a reason to come back to class every week.

The more we enjoyed thinking about the future, the more Buon detested the idea. When the whole class laughed out loud at the mundane fish sauce burger, Buon was quiet and kept to himself. Mrs. Winona asked him to join and share with the class, but he just kept looking at his feet and didn't speak to anyone. He became more depressed as the days passed. During class when I encouraged him to write down, "What I will do when I settle in another country?" he cocooned himself and ignored me. He didn't bother to pay attention. He just kicked at the floor.

One afternoon I finally reached a point where I couldn't handle Buon ignoring me any longer so I patted him on the back and asked him to stop. To my surprise, he stood up and walked out of the classroom. I ran after him and called out his name, but he yelled to leave him alone. I went back to class feeling rejected. Mrs. Winona came over and told me that I couldn't help him anymore. He had to help himself.

What happened after Buon ran out of the class shocked us all. Mrs. Winona arrived the next day with tears in her eyes. She sat at her desk and cried for a long time. We all anticipated that something horrible had happened, something that was causing our beloved teacher to sob her heart out. After a long silence Mrs. Winona composed herself and stood up, and with great effort she told us that Buon was dead.

My world went dark and I lost my hearing. How could he die? You stupid idiot! You can't die! You're supposed to go on and live the life your parents sacrificed themselves for. You're a coward. You took the easy way out. You were among the children of Heaven, and you had to be strong like our ancestors. They fought the Chinese and they fought the French, both powerful enemies. They never quit, ever, and here you lost only your family and you quit. I hate quitters.

And then seemingly out of the dark corner of my subconscious mind, I could hear the laughter of the Sea Devil. It chuckled in satisfaction and told me to let it out of the box. It demanded that I follow in my friend's footsteps and think of the past, think of the suffering as if it were the key to unleashing it from the prison where I kept it locked up. "Let me out," it screamed and shouted at me. I covered my ears, but I could still hear it speaking to me. "Why live in a world with such sorrow? Come and visit your friend. Buon is right here. He has released himself from all suffering. You should too."

The box tempted me. It was right. Why live to endure such painful experiences, I asked myself. The voice inside the box was getting louder and I could sense the devil was getting stronger. As I let my guard down, the chains that I had wrapped around it were about to be broken free. With just another strong push it would be all over. I would follow Buon, and see him on the other side. I would run to the forbidden beach and jump off a cliff. I stood up and was moving toward the door to follow through with this when a sudden shake brought me to my senses. Standing in front of me was Master.

"Are you all right?" she inquired. Without waiting for an answer, she hugged me and I held her tight in my arms. Like the sun peeking out from the gray sky, the warmth of her love overtook my body. It calmed the Sea Devil inside the box. I realized that if I ever let the demon inside this box free it would cost me my life. I took the opportunity and put a wall around it, a survival mechanism, with the hope that it would be strong enough to contain the darkness inside me.

Life went on, but its rhythm changed. It could never be the same with the knowledge that a friend you had cared deeply about had put a rope around his neck and jumped off a cliff. Dangling in mid-air, he had swung back and forth like a goodbye that was never meant to be. After he was gone I cared little about leaving this prison. But sometimes mysterious powers have other ideas.

It was late afternoon and I was busy cleaning fish in the kitchen when a voice came over the speaker announcing important news. The administrative office informed us that a Canadian delegate would be in camp tomorrow and the applications to Canada would be handed out first thing, at 7 a.m.

At dinner I told Tan about the news and we both agreed we should apply because any place would better than here.

I woke that morning and followed my usual routine—brushed my teeth, grabbed my books, and headed to school. The sun had started to warm up and the little market was already bustling with people going about their business, trading and selling goods. I felt like a new journey was about to begin.

I saw Master in her usual spot in the front row of the class. She looked up as I walked in, astonished by my presence.

"What are you doing here?" she asked.

"Last time I checked, I go to school here," I replied sarcastically.

"Aren't you supposed to line up at the administrative office for the Canadian delegates?"

"My brother is there this morning," I replied.

"I didn't see him when I walked by on my way to school," Master told me.

Immediately, I got up and dashed toward the administrative office. People were lined up at the door and circled around it. I lined up behind an elderly woman who turned and smiled at me. In politeness I smiled back, hoping I was not too late. I scanned the line for my brother, but he was nowhere in sight. A few minutes later, the line started to move. Inside the house the petite young woman behind the desk asked for my name and birth date. She wrote my information on what seemed like an application, then looked up at me and asked where my guardians were. I told her he was busy. She said if I didn't come back with him within an hour, my application would be considered forfeit.

I galloped out of the door and back to the house to look for Tan. I inspected the complex inside and out, but found no trace of him. Angrily, I marched toward his friend's place and inquired about Tan's whereabouts. He told me he had seen him going up the mountain. The thought of not having an interview for the application to Canada and being stuck even longer on this island gave me the energy to run across the camp and up the hill through the mountain trail to the spot where we usually gathered fresh water.

I climbed a boulder the size of a house, tormented by the thought of missing the interview and dying like Buon on this island. I was exhausted but eventually I reached the top. There stood my brother, naked, showering and singing, like a kid with no worries and no recollection of what he had promised. I yelled his name to get his attention. He turned around and looked at me and I watched his eyes as it dawned on him where he was supposed to be.

We barely made it in time for our interview. My brother and I were rushed to a small office, the same one where we had the last interview. The vomit smell still lingered in the air. A tall, slim man with a mustache and a kind face stepped in a few minutes later and introduced himself in Vietnamese as Paul, an immigration officer from Canada. He sat down on the wooden chair across from us and looked from me to Tan. His gaze lingered on Tan, probably wondering why he was at such an important interview in his shorts and a tank top, soaking wet.

Paul asked us for our names and birth dates. He spent a few minutes asking about my brother's background and what kind of job experience he had. Tan struggled with English so much that Paul resorted to speaking to him in Vietnamese. He asked Tan, "Why do you want to come to Canada?"

Tan looked at me for a moment and I never thought he would answer the way he did, but thinking about it after all these years I'm not surprised. My older brother, the one that I looked up to, looked at Paul and after a few moments said that he had heard Canada was like America—it had the most beautiful women in the world and it was for this reason alone that he wanted to go.

Paul stared at Tan and composed his thoughts, taking his time to digest the information. Without a word, he turned to look at me. I thought the interview was over and that he was going to stand up and shoo us out the door, telling us Canada would be the last country that we would ever settle in. But no. Paul burst into hysterical laughter. Tan then followed, laughing his heart out. Paul patted Tan's shoulder and said that he was funny.

There I was, sitting with two grown men laughing about Brother's heartfelt reason to immigrate to Canada. I mustered a fake laugh to try and share the joke. Paul put on a stern expression and looked at me. In English he asked what I was going to do once I arrived in Canada. I remembered that in class Mrs. Winona had told me that immigration officers like to test young children on their English-speaking skills and if they couldn't pass, the application would be rejected.

I stared at Paul, drawing a blank. With so much anxiety I couldn't think properly. I was a frozen statue. Paul repeated his question in case I hadn't heard it the first time. Silence stretched on, and I knew I needed to find an answer quickly. Tan kicked my foot and I remembered Master's dream. "Social worker," I blurted out.

No comments of any kind, Paul closed our file, gave us a little smile and announced that our results would be published on the administrative office bulletin board tomorrow. He stood up and walked us out of the office. I wanted to ask him to give me another chance. I wanted to tell him I hadn't been prepared for the question that was why I'd hesitated, but Paul didn't look at me. Tan could see that I wanted to run back, but he pushed me along.

That night I lay awake thinking about the question. There were millions of answers I could have given. If I could have just made up my mind, I could have told him I wanted to be a doctor or a lawyer, like many kids in my class would have said. I should have told him I wanted to be a journalist or a writer. I started to condemn myself for being such a bumbling idiot. I prayed to ancestors for help and provide me with the energy and the spirit to accept whatever the next day might hold. I desperately needed to leave this island. My stomach growled and I prayed, nursing myself to sleep.

The day after the interview, I woke long before the sun rose and rushed to the administrative office, hoping to see my name. When I got there, I quickly grabbed the posting and scanned it for Manh Tran, but to no avail. I had failed. I cursed and damned myself. I felt sorry for having to live and endure the hopelessness of this wasteland.

Holding the paper in my hands, I wondered how much longer I could live on this island that was worse than death. We were being constantly woken by screams of terrors at night. Robberies, murder, and theft had become constant occurrences to the point that when the sun set, people hid in their houses. The bloodshed scared me. A week prior to the interview, a fight had broken out while I stood in line for rations. In front of me, an orphan boy about fifteen years of age had stabbed another boy in the stomach for cutting in line. His blood painted the sand red. A month earlier, a man smashed a woman on the head with a rock because she wouldn't work for him as a prostitute. Fear that someday Brother or I could be the next victim often made me shiver at night, especially when a scream from nearby echoed in the air. I couldn't handle living like this anymore. I thought again have doing what Buon had done—making a quick exit.

After checking the results and not seeing my name, I became very depressed. I stayed in the library all day. At dinner, Brother looked at my upside-down smile and asked what was wrong. I replied that we would continue to live here.

"That's really too bad. You can stay, but as for me, I'm leaving," Tan said sarcastically. I couldn't contain my excitement. I jumped up and ran back to the administrative office to check again. There it was … *Tan Tran* … the most beautiful letters in the history of any language appeared before my eyes. Unbeknownst to me, results were posted under the guardian's first name. I had been searching for the wrong name all along.

We were notified that our departure date was three days away, and with that information came a number of emotions. First was the realization of leaving this temporary shelter. I had wanted to leave so badly, but now I couldn't stand the thought of not seeing Master, Mrs. Winona and my other friends. They were the people who helped me through the many dark nights at camp. They were my comrades in hunger and in tears. I began to miss them terribly.

Second was my apprehension over the unknown. I kept trying to picture what Canada would be like. Mrs. Winona warned me it was a very cold place with lots of snow. Based on that, I thought Canada would be one of those places with snow all year round and Brother and I would live in an igloo. It would be cold and uncomfortable.

Third, I was concerned about Tan's well being. I didn't know if he would be all right in Canada. He had told me many times that he didn't want to go anywhere but home, but my worries subsided a little when he told me he would work hard so he could sponsor the rest of our family to come to Canada. All I had to worry about was school, he said, so when our mother came she would be proud of us.

I asked Tan then what he knew of our family situation back home. He shook his head and left me to my own thoughts and headed outside for a smoke. After a few minutes, he left to go drink.

For three days I searched for Master to say goodbye, but she seemed to have disappeared. I stopped by her home and her uncle told me that she had gone somewhere. I checked the usual spots we visited without any luck.

As our final moments on the island drew near, I stood at the gate leading to the dock, where a high-speed boat was waiting, hoping to see Master. The waves were beating against the shore like a goodbye from Bidong, the island that had sheltered me for more than three years. I had dreamed about this day for a long, long time. Now I was almost hesitant to leave because along with the pain there were also fond memories.

Master came out of the crowd to say goodbye. I could see tears streaking down her face, but she tried to hold them in. I stood there holding myself together with every muscle of my body, knowing that if I just looked at her, I too would be in tears. I looked at the sand. I wanted to tell Master to take care of herself and that I would miss her, but the words got stuck in my throat and didn't want to come out. Master came closer, gave me a kiss on the cheek and handed me a present. I concentrated long and hard and finally was able to pull from my pocket the letter I had written for her.

Dear Luly,

Here is a poem from me to you, something that no money could buy.

Goodbye my friend, it's time to say goodbye
The times we left behind were sublime
We had fun in the sun; we had joy in the sand
We had a hard time leaving our native land

Goodbye my friend, it's time to say goodbye
I will take this memory with me for a lifetime
I will remember the times we shared, and laugh
I will remember the times we cried and endured

Goodbye my friend, it's time to say goodbye
I will carry with me the picture of you,
To the new land that I do not know
I will miss you so much it hurts.

Goodbye my friend, it's time to say goodbye
I leave you with many kind words left behind
Wishing you the best that life has to offer
Wishing you find what you are looking for
Wishing you the very best, and more.

Goodbye my friend, it's time to say goodbye.

We boarded the speedboat and it quickly took Brother and me away. I kept looking back searching for Master, but I couldn't see her anywhere in the crowd. I kept searching long after the island disappeared into the horizon.

Chapter 12

Ming domination, Posterior Trần, & Later Lê dynasties (1407 – 1527)

In 1407, under the pretext of helping to restore the Trần Dynasty, Chinese Ming troops invaded Đại Ngu and captured Hồ Quý Ly and Hồ Hán Thương. The Hồ Dynasty came to an end after only 7 years in power.

After a two-hour boat ride through the rough seas, we huddled on a tour bus for another eight hours as it snaked through the mountains of Malaysia. Growing up in a village, I had never taken a bus, and motion sickness hit me quickly. The egg salad and apple juice given to me by the Red Crescent left my stomach almost as soon as it entered. The driver felt sorry for me and stopped by the road and brought me some pills. I took them and for hours afterward I felt like I was in a dream, half asleep and half awake, until the bus stopped in front of a gated community. It was called Sungei Besi and was a temporary processing center set up by the United Nations High Commissioner for Refugees to hold those waiting for medical clearance.

Sungei Besi was located in the capital city of Malaysia, Kuala Lumpur. It was a very small camp compared to Bidong, consisting of twenty houses surrounding a medical center and school. The houses were outfitted with a bed on each side of the wall and a desk with a small lamp for studying.

Next to the entrance of the camp were the administration offices and a housing complex for the doctors and volunteers. There was also a twenty-four hour cafeteria. Because of the location and proximity to the capital city, Sungei Besi had been a well-equipped and well-fed refugee camp. I was given three meals a day, often rich foods like pizza, spaghetti, and cheese. Snacks were brought to school and children got extra meals.

This was the first time I was exposed to the North American style of excess. There was more food than I could stuff into my belly, and every day I ate until it ached. After being without food for such a long time in Bidong, I became obsessed with hoarding food. I would take more than I could eat in a single serving and secretly bring it back to the house. This was forbidden for fear of infestation, but I didn't know any better. I hid the food under the bed and put it under clothes. I ate it a few days later, but two-day-old fried chicken and french fries were not healthy things to be eating no matter how tasty they once were. I was so sick I had to be taken to the emergency room. That was the last secret food stashing that I kept!

The more I grew to love western food, the more Brother hated it. He complained constantly about anything that didn't resemble fish sauce or watercress. The gap between my brother and me widened as time went on. Food preferences were just the tip of the iceberg.

School was set up in a manner whereby everyone had to attend, just as they would in Canada. The lessons were designed to teach us what it meant to be Canadian and what was expected of us there.

The class began with the geography of Canada. Compared to the rest of the world, Canada had a very large landmass but less than 25 million souls to occupy it. Most cities were located near the border of the United States, as though Canadians secretly wanted to be Americans. After being in Canada for many years, I now know this is not the case. Canadians settled close to the border so Americans don't have to travel as far to visit their neighbors. Canadians are such nice people that it's only natural we would think about other people first.

At the end of each class, we were introduced to North American cinema. The class instructor screened *Star Wars* and I was hooked immediately. I saw myself as Luke Skywalker, the Jedi Knight. I could relate to the idea that he was forced to leave home. I saw my school as the training camp where Skywalker had to train every day to strengthen his power of The Force. For me, the force of education had trained my mind. Our classroom became the battleground between The Galactic Alliance and The Rebellion led by yours truly. I daydreamed of training with Master Yoda and becoming a full-fledged Jedi Knight to save my own Princess Leia in the Bidong refugee camp, the one who had kissed me before I left.

The most appealing thing the instructor told me was that in Canada there were places with lots of books on many different subjects. You could read as much as your heart desired. I imagined spending all day at such a place. I would sleep there until I could digest all the volumes of books. Back in my village such a place would be unthinkable.

I embraced the thought of living in Canada, the opportunities and the lifestyle I would have. I began to speak English more and more often with friends and classmates, telling them that we should practice since we would soon be Canadian.

At home I encouraged Tan to practice too. I asked him to speak with me but he lashed out at the idea as though I had insulted him. He went on to tell me how great and deep the Vietnamese language was. I defended myself. I told him that since we were going to be Canadians, it would be best that we speak and act like one. He told me that if I wanted to become a stupid Canadian I would have to do it on my own. Then he slammed his chair back with a bang and walked angrily out of the house. I thought he was angry because his English was weak and he was self-conscious, so I didn't take his hostility to heart. In his heart, the power of darkness was too great for my little power of The Force to penetrate, and Master Yoda hadn't yet shown me how to do mind-control so I couldn't change his thoughts.

After that argument, the atmosphere at home changed. I spoke to Tan in English and then translated to Vietnamese, hoping he might pick up a few words here and there. I wanted to become a Canadian so much that I went to the cafeteria and began to order sandwiches, spaghetti and pizza instead of traditional Vietnamese meals like rice and fish. I also started going to English-speaking services at church. Like a dried sponge, I began to soak up the culture of the country where I would soon settle.

I listened to and enjoyed the CBC on a radio that Master and Mrs. Winona had given to me as a present when I left Bidong. I learned of many world events like the end to the Cold War, the United States lifting trade sanctions against China, and the many uprisings and deaths that followed the official closing of our refugee camp. I treasured that radio and kept it next to the bed, turning it on at every opportunity.

Fascination with western values brought me great happiness, but my beloved brother thought otherwise. He didn't have the patience to learn English in the classes held by the Canadian government. He left ten minutes into the first session. He found like-minded people and continued to drink. He often started when he woke up and didn't finish until late in the night.

While I was studying, engulfing in a new culture, he was drowning in alcohol. I looked forwarded to a new beginning, while he held on to his old traditions and ideas. The space between us was getting wider and wider, but we were too blind to see it or do anything about it.

One day about five months after settling in Sengei Besi, when I was busy doing my homework on the bed, Tan stumbled home from a day of drinking with his buddies. He came zigzagging toward me, staring at me like a hungry dog and asked, "You little root-forgetter, what are you doing?" His alcohol breath sprayed me in the face.

"I am doing my homework," I replied, not bothering to look at him. "You should go to bed," I added.

He didn't hear my comments and pressed on. "Root forgetter!" he mocked again before taking another drink from his bottle. "You have forgotten your Vietnamese roots." He spoke to me in a very harsh tone, trying to intimidate me.

But I wasn't afraid. With my proper English and with my foreign friends, I felt superior to Brother. What a stupid thought. "I'm learning about a language and culture that I will soon be living in, unlike you. You keep on drinking." I matched the rise in volume that he dished out. I felt anger toward this drunkard for putting me down. "Vietnam is no longer our country. We are stateless." I showed him our refugee cards, with STATELESS in bold letters, proving to Tan that we were no longer Vietnamese.

Fired by my defiance, Tan rose up. He pointed a finger at my face and said, "You are a dumbass, dimwitted root-forgetter. You are no Canadian. You are worthless, you are nothing. And you want to be Canadian?" He had never used such language with me, and I was shocked.

"So what if I want to be Canadian? What are you going to do about it?" I replied in anger.

His face turned even redder at my rebellion. What followed happened so quickly that I didn't see it coming. I only felt the hard slap across my face. The jolt threw me to the ground. I quickly stood up, caressing my face to soothe the pain. I looked at him defiantly, with bulging eyes, squeezing my fists trying to calm myself. He picked up the radio that was given to me by my best friend and teacher, the only thing that reminded me of them, and tossed it to the ground. It broke apart and its plastic pieces scattered all over the floor. "I am your older brother. I will teach you a lesson," he screamed at me.

I wanted to fight back, but Father taught me never to hit my siblings. Brother had forgotten that lesson, but I did not and never would, because it was a gift from Father.

A voice came from outside. I turned and saw that a few people had gathered to see what was happening. They scattered when I noticed them. I was filled with anger and I was afraid this was going to get worse, so I bolted out the door. I ran as long as I could, and then walked aimlessly until I settled on a swing near the school. I felt hurt and humiliated by Brother. I questioned why he would say and do what he did. We were stateless, but Canada would soon be our home. He needed to embrace our new country, as I had.

Sitting on the swing rubbing the necklace Mother had given me, I thought back to the many life lessons she had taught me. In the end, I told myself that Tan was just drunk and I should not hold a grudge, as my parents had taught me. Satisfied with the answers I had found, I walked home.

Tan was snoring in bed when I crept in. I cleaned up the radio and wondered how long it would be before I could afford to buy a new one. And, like I did many times in my life, I put those sad and scary memories in a box and moved on like nothing had ever happened.

After six months at Sengei Besi and after passing all the health tests, the Canadian government sent us a package containing our airplane tickets to Canada. I was jubilant by the news and hoped a change of scenery would help Tan and mend our relationship. I hurried to pack all of my belongings: three t-shirts and two pairs of stitched-up shorts.

I said goodbye to friends, wearing ragged-but-good-enough shirt and too-long pants, the best clothes I had in my possessions.

Knowing that this would be the last time I saw the temporary camp, I tried to take a mental picture that I could carry with me the rest of my life. That picture reminded me of hope, the hope that came with moving to a new country - it would be tough but it would eventually be better for those of us who could adapt.

Chapter 13

Divided period (1527 – 1802)

The Lê dynasty was overthrown by its general named Mạc Đăng Dung in 1527. He killed the Lê emperor and proclaimed himself emperor, starting the Mạc Dynasty.

We arrived in Canada on September 18, 1992 and were greeted with a chilly afternoon in Medicine Hat, Alberta.

A bus arranged by social services took us from the airport to the social housing complex on the corner of 4th Street and 5th Avenue South East. We rode along the well-paved streets past shopping malls and glassed office buildings. In my fourteen-year-old head, I was a child going to school for the first time, full of awe and fascination. I stared with admiration at these technological advancements of human civilization. I had never thought such well-structured traffic and such a clean city existed in the world. I felt like I was in Heaven. I pointed at the many beautiful automobiles that passed by, dumbstruck at how orderly it all was. Tan didn't seem to care for it one bit. He just nodded his head slightly in acknowledgment. He seemed cold and distant, but I didn't give much thought to it.

Half an hour later, the bus stopped in front of a tall, gray brick building with windows facing every direction. The building contained twelve floors with 120 residential units. Brother and I were introduced to our home. Our apartment was on the first floor, with big windows in the living room looking out to the street. The kitchen was on the right with beige cabinets. The walls were painted vanilla throughout the apartment.

I was astonished by the appliances in the apartment, like the 19-inches television, the refrigerator, and the electric stove. I looked at the sofa like a man looks at an exotic creature and ran my hand along the smooth fabric. I touched the cushion as Adam touching Eve for the very first time. After about ten minutes of careful inspection, Tan looked at me and signaled that it would be safe to sit on it. I stepped back and offered him the opportunity to try it first. He turned around slowly and started to rest his bottom, then immediately stood up. “What’s the matter?” I asked. He complained that something was wrong with the sofa. “It’s sinking,” he said. We looked and inspected it to make sure there wasn’t a hole beneath the seat. After another ten minutes of cautious examination, we sat down and enjoyed our first piece of Canadian luxury: the lazy chair.

Of all the rooms in the apartment, the one that was most puzzling was the room with the water hole. There was a small ceramic bowl, filled about halfway with water and at the back of it another bowl with a handle sticking out on the left side, when pulled a hissing sound startled us. We stood back and took cover, preparing for something to explode, and wondered why these westerners would put something so dangerous inside their house. The water swirled and disappeared before filling the bowl again. We were left speechless by such luxury.

Imagine having a water well built right into your house waiting to be used!

We would still be using the water well for our daily needs if not for Thomas, our social worker, who came by our apartment the next day and saw us taking the water from our well to offer him a drink. When he saw Tan use a cup to scoop the water from the well to give him, he stopped us mid track. He looked at us with amusement and understanding. Thomas showed us the intended purpose of our water well. Tan and I excused ourselves and for the next hour we scrubbed ourselves from top to bottom, inside and out. I put soap in my mouth and rinsed multiple times. I washed and rewashed myself until my body began to bruise and bleed. Thomas further helped us to navigate around our new world by showing how to use the other appliances such as the microwave, the oven and the electric stove.

Thomas walked us to his car, a blue four-door Ford Focus. He drove us a few blocks to a bank and gave us $550 as a monthly allowance from the social welfare office. With Thomas's help, we opened our first bank account and he showed us how to use the ATM machine. Settling into the McDonald's restaurant next door for lunch, I devoured a Big Mac and a Coke. Tan, however, only took a few bites and handed me his to finish.

While having lunch, Thomas explained how to use the bus system by showing us his transit map. He pointed out where the bus stops were and how to pay for the service. Much of what Thomas said I had to translate for Tan because his language skills were only good enough to carry on a simple conversation. I had encouraged Tan to practice and learn English with the hope that he would improve, but he was stubborn and hadn't the patience to do it. Before departing, Thomas took us to a grocery store to help us stock up on food and kitchen supplies. We were very grateful to Thomas for his help and invited him to stay for dinner. He declined, but promised to come back the next day to show me how to get to school.

I lay in the dark room listening to Tan tossing and turning in his bed, unable to sleep. He complained that the bed was too soft and fought it for about fifteen minutes before taking his blanket and pillow and settling to sleep on the floor. That night, excited about going to school, I made a promise to myself that I would study hard so that I could one day bring my family to Canada, then Mother and Sister wouldn't have to work in the fields anymore. I would become a highly paid professional and we would live in a big house. I would drive a car like Thomas and eat in great restaurants like McDonalds.

Early the next morning I was awoken by a sound from the kitchen. I lazily walked out to investigate. I saw Tan packing a bowl of rice and some boiled eggs in a bag. I asked him what he was doing, and he explained that he was off to look for a job. With his lunch and some city street maps, he headed out the door.

Half an hour later, Thomas showed up at the apartment and drove me to McCoy High School. I was introduced to Miss Stern, the school counselor. After a few pleasantries, Thomas left, wishing me luck. Miss Stern was a slim woman with thick round glasses. She took me to the cafeteria, gave me a pencil and a stack of papers and told me I would be tested to determine my learning level and grade. After an hour she came back, took me to her office and had me wait for another half hour before taking me to the grade 10 teacher.

Mrs. Daneila was a fairly young woman, with a snow-white complexion, plump body, and a dimpled smile. She introduced herself to me as my homeroom teacher and showed me to my seat at the far left of the room, next to a boy around my age with curly blond hair, who later introduced himself as Duane. As I sat down the bell rang, signaling the end of first period. I looked at my schedule and walked slowly, trying to navigate the sea of students crisscrossing the hallway. Duane was very helpful. Without him as my guide, I am sure I would still be lost in one of the many classrooms at McCoy High School.

At the end of the first day of school, I lugged my textbooks home with the thought I should at least try to catch up using the available material. The books were thick and I had a hard time carrying them. Again, Duane offered to help. We walked home together and he took the time to show me the park where kids usually hung out and recommended I hang out there sometime, but I didn't much care for the idea as educations was foremost in my mind.

For the first couple of weeks, Tan had a hard time finding a job, even though he was very persistent. He woke up early every day without fail, packed his lunch, grabbed a map and wandered the streets of Medicine Hat looking for work. He would often come home exhausted, eat silently, and head out to have a cigarette before bed. We didn't have much conversation. I would do my homework and he would watch TV. On the weekends, I spent my days in the library focused on my studies, after which, I would go home, cook dinner, eat, read a book and go to bed. Both of us had a role to play and we just followed what was expected of us.

Late one Sunday as I stumbled out of bed to get a drink of water, I saw that Tan's bed was empty. It was five minutes past midnight. Worried, I went out to check for him, but there was no sign that he had been home. Was he lost? Did he get into an accident? My mind started to move a hundred miles a minute with worry. Then the door jerked open and Tan stumbled in. He steadied himself against the wall, walked to the sofa, lied down, and fell asleep. I took a blanket and covered him for fear he might catch a cold and went back to bed.

I awoke early the next morning and readied myself for school. I looked at the sofa but didn't see Tan there. He must have gone out looking for a job early again, I thought. I put on my clothes, picked up my bag, and headed out the door. I saw Tan on the other side of the street, at the bus stop. I called out to him and he turned around, waved at me and smiled. I rushed over.

"Hi, Brother. Where are you going so early in the morning?" I asked.

"I'm going to work," he said, beaming with the confidence of a man who could support his brother.

"You found work? That's good news. Where?" I asked in excitement.

"At an Italian restaurant about an hour's bus ride from here. As a busboy. Don't cook tonight. I will bring us back some food." He hurried to get onto the bus.

That night, we had a feast of restaurant leftovers. I was baffled by the amount of food that was being wasted. We gorged on a big chicken thigh that had been marinated and grilled to perfection and a steak that had never been touched. We ate so much food that our stomachs ached, but we couldn't bear to see it wasted so we lay in the living room and took turns devouring the throwaway until our stomachs could not handle any more. Then we fought over the use of the washroom.

The end of the month came and Thomas showed up at our apartment. I had just arrived home from school and he greeted me in his respectful manner. I asked him to come in and have some water. While sitting at our dining table, he pulled out a check and handed it to me saying, "Here is your social assistance money to help you through the coming month."

I looked at him, then the check. I picked it up in my hands and then returned it to Thomas.

"Thank you, Thomas. My brother and I are grateful for this country that has helped us so much. He has found a job and I am sure we can support ourselves with it."

"Oh. What kind of job did he find?" Thomas asked excitedly.

"A busboy at an Italian restaurant," I answered with much enthusiasm.

"That's good news. I'm glad you two have made such a great start."

After a few casual remarks, Thomas said goodbye and walked back to his car. That night, I told Tan the story and he concurred with my decision. Tan took out a stack of dollar bills and showed me his check. I counted while he was in the shower. His wages more than covered our rent and meals for the month. I was quite happy that a busboy could make so much money. I commented to Tan that Canada was a wonderful place, and he looked at me for a brief moment before giving a hint of a smile full of self-assurance.

It was blissful in the early days settling Canada. Learning through Thomas that we could sponsor our family, I counted the days until we could see Mother and Sister again. With Brother's job, I was sure we could save enough money to hire a lawyer and commence the sponsorship process. The harder I studied, the easier it came. So I set a goal for myself—to study as hard as I could so that when Mother arrived she would be happy. I was resolute from that day forward about reuniting our family one day.

Chapter 14

Trịnh & Nguyễn lords

In the year 1600, Nguyễn Hoàng also declared himself Lord (officially "Vương", popularly "Chúa") and refused to send more money or soldiers to help the Trịnh. He also moved his capital to Phú Xuân, modern-day Huế. Nguyễn Hoàng died in 1613 after having ruled the south for 55 years.

Ten months into school, I had already made great strides. I had many friends, I had joined the hockey team, and I was making money through having a paper route.

Among the many friends was Jennifer, a girl who lived in the same building as us. She and her family were from Russia and had been in Canada for three years. She was the oldest sibling of four. She had long blond hair and a fair complexion with many freckles on her slender face. She and I often walked home together.

We weren't in the same class but we had the same math teacher, Mr. Weiss, a math whiz who danced around the most complicated equations with ease. It was difficult, however, to ask him to explain a solution in detail because he had a stutter, so going through even a simple problem could be very hard to understand and very time consuming. Jennifer and I often spent the evening in my apartment doing homework together. Her math skills needed improvement so I began showing her basic math, from multiplication tables and fractions to functions.

In return for tutoring, Jennifer showed me around town. The first place she took me to was the Medicine Hat Mall. As I stepped off the bus and walked through the revolving glass doors, I was greeted by an ocean of pedestrians. People were everywhere, pushing and heading in all directions, like a village living inside the building. Stores were brightly lit and colorfully decorated, and the sparkling light, which bathed the many mannequins in tightly fit clothes, invited me to come in.

I was amazed by the beautiful displays surrounding me and stupefied by the sheer number of stores, appearing one after the other with clothes stacked tightly on the racks. I looked at myself in a mirror. I saw a tall, slender, stick figure with protruding eyes and bushy eyebrows topped with a head full of thick black hair. I was wearing an old ragged t-shirt and pants that appeared to have been worn far more than they should have been. With Jennifer's help, I purchased new clothes.

Jennifer and I took turns trying on many fancy outfits. She modeled for me and I for her. We walked the catwalk in $1000 skirts or Armani suits that were far too expensive for us but still fun to try on. I picked up a briefcase and pretended to walk like a banker. Jennifer said I looked good in a beige blazer and I told her she looked good in a mini skirt. We tested a new Sealy numbered mattress, a new La-Z-Boy sofa, and lounged in front of a humongous television. It was amazing. We pretended it was our house until the manager and security escorted us out of the store and told us never to come back.

From my paper route, I saved up enough money to buy Tan a Roots winter jacket and leather gloves for Christmas. In exchange, he gave me a box of underwear. I thought it was funny at first, but he told me that I was a growing boy and I should start thinking about girls. My face turned red, and I told him that we should not talk about such things, that we should be thinking about our family.

I wrote home to tell our family that Brother and I had settled in Canada and we would soon sponsor them to come over. I wrote more than a dozen times, but all of the letters were returned. I was distraught and began to wonder what was happening to them back home. But as I had done often enough before, I sealed those worries away and continued living my life, afraid to find out the truth. I believed that the present and future were constant, and I shut out the past, pretending it never existed.

Brother was the only part of my life that reminded me who I was and, at times, I secretly pretended he did not exist as well because every time I thought of where I came from I was ashamed of abandoning my roots. To make matters worse, the Sea Devil kept knocking at the door of my subconscious, ready to take over my body if I strayed from my busy life. Thoughts of home and what had happened during the escape from Vietnam and at Bidong were too much for me. I had subconsciously created a system of safeguarding myself from the many hurtful memories, so strong that they might kill me if I ever let them escape. I changed my name to Manny and sealed away the old.

Duane and Jennifer reminded me of Master and Buon, both of whom I thought about on nights when I couldn't sleep. I was glad to have friends, because without them, life in Canada would have been very lonely. Tan, on the other hand, hadn't made any friends and was very lonely. He went to work, then came home to his television and his beer. He drank until he fell asleep. When he woke up, the cycle would start again.

School and activities like hockey and hanging out with friends gradually became my priorities. My conversations with Tan became more and more rare, until they seemed to end altogether. The apartment became cold and unwelcoming. I went home only to sleep, nothing more. Whenever I thought of Tan and our relationship, I told myself that we were simply busy, he with his work, trying to save up to sponsor our family, and I, with my education.

A year went by quickly as Tan and I tried to integrate ourselves into Canadian society. Being young and agile had made it easy for me, but Tan had a hard time. Reunion with our family had been our top priority and the only thing to which Tan was desperately looking forward. But making it happen wasn't as easy as we thought.

I walked into the apartment one day and Tan was home early with a beer in one hand, the other holding the remote flipping through the TV channels. He was a little buzzed and he looked at me with a dull face. I greeted him and headed to the kitchen in search of food. I opened the fridge full of Budweiser and thought, "wow, he must really love that stuff." I put water into a pot and opened a bag of noodles for my dinner. I sat next to Tan on the sofa with the cup of noodles in my hand and we started to talk. He told me he went to the immigration office earlier that day to learn about the process of sponsoring our family, and found that in order to qualify we would need an income of close to $70,000 annually—a lot of money. With my brother's busboy job and my paper route we would never have that kind of income. I told Tan I could help, that I would quit school and get a job. Tan stopped me immediately. He wanted none of that. Besides, what would I do? Get another busboy job? We still wouldn't have enough.

The day of reunion with our family was drifting further and further away from us and there seemed to be no light at the end of the tunnel. The thought that I would never see my family again rolled around in my head. I felt so lonely. I sat next to Tan for comfort. Seeing him made me feel I wasn't alone in this world. We sat together for a long time. Neither of us spoke a word, as if we understood that we were the only ones left. Tan finished a dozen more beers and started mumbling to himself. I could hear him saying that he hated this country. He hated the cold in the winter and the boiling heat in the summer. He thought white people were stupid and they didn't understand what he said.

I felt sorry for Tan but I didn't know what to say. Tired from the sad news, I decided to head to bed. Tan picked himself up and went to the fridge for another beer. He tried to open the cap, but it seemed too stubborn. He got more and more agitated and tried using his teeth to loosen the cap, but his tooth was chipped in the process and it began to bleed. The pain shot through his body and he screamed loudly. He threw the bottle at the floor then took another bottle and threw it against the wall, cursing the country the way a gambler curses at luck for not being on his side. When he finished throwing the beer bottles he started on the dishes. Every shattered piece of our dinnerware was accompanied by a line about how Canada was a country for idiots, for bastards, and for losers.

When he didn't have anything left to throw, he broke down and cried. Tan never cried. Never had I seen him so weak, not when Father had nearly killed him, nor when Mr. Toi had disgraced him, nor when he longed for his wife. He was a man's man. But he had turned into a creature that felt lonely and out of place in the world that was not his.

I helped him to his bed then went to clean up. What a mess, I thought to myself. Why did he keep putting these poisons in his system? Where was the fun in it? I could never figure out why so many people enjoyed drinking. Can they really find escape? I tried his beer once. It had tasted nasty and bitter like fermented water that normal people would have just thrown out.

I swept all the broken glass into the dustpan and threw it into the waste container outside. Back in the apartment, I could hear Tan snoring. It sounded like he was deep in sleep. I thought about what Tan had said earlier and our inability to sponsor our family as I mopped the floor. I felt so isolated from our ancestors. I called out to Mother under my breath, then to Father and Sister to ease the pain and loneliness in my heart. I felt like I had been deserted on this earth. I wanted to go home to the rice farm and to the coconut house that leaked during the rain and smelled of raisins. The thought that I would never see them again hurt to the bone, like winter that never went away.

At the age of fifteen, I was a man without a parent in a foreign country that I now called my own. Vietnam would no longer accept me. I had left it, abandoning my birthright. I was a traitor to my own kind. I was no longer Vietnamese, so what had I become?

The rain came again into my life. I tried to hold it off. I told it to go away. I even sang the song that I heard in the refugee camp: *Rain, rain, go away, come again another day*. The rain never did go away. The harder I fought it, the stronger it brought forth sad memories of Mother, Father, and Sister into my mind.

Once again, through experience and persistence, I found myself filing these feelings away under the deep ocean floor. I told myself that in order to live, I needed to keep the emptiness locked up and never look at it because it hurt too much to think about. I was too fragile and weak to realize my true self. I knew if I ever opened the emotions inside of me, it would hit me like Niagara Falls, with a force so strong it would destroy me like it had destroyed Tan.

After cleaning up the mess Brother made, I started my homework as though nothing had happened. In my mind, my studies remained my focus. The future was a variable and the past was just an existing, unstable formula, nothing more. The present was what I lived by.

Chapter 15

Advent of the Europeans & southward expansion

The West's exposure in Vietnam and Vietnam's exposure to Westerners dated back to 166 AD with the arrival of merchants from the Roman Empire, to 1292 with the visit of Marco Polo, and the early 16th century with the arrival of Portuguese in 1516 and other European traders and missionaries.

Life changed drastically after we learned that our family would forever be apart. Brother and I lived like ghosts, as if each of us reminded the other of pain and suffering. We stayed away from each other. Brother came home late at night and went to work very early in the morning. On the weekends and on his days off, I lived at the library, only coming home to sleep. We barely saw one another and we spoke even less. The house became colder and darker as we drifted into two different worlds, out of touch with each other. We lived as if parts of us were missing, but life went on. I was busy with school and he was busy with his job, and three years went by in an instant.

High school graduation was fast approaching and since my grades were excellent, applying to university was easy. As a child, I had always wanted to write, and becoming a journalist was a logical choice. With the help of Miss Stern I applied to the University of Saskatchewan, thinking that it was not only close to home, additionally Duane would also be there to help me along the way.

A letter of acceptance arrived a few week later. I held onto it, wondering how to break the news to Tan. I was the only relative he had. If I were to abandon him, how would I ever live with myself? Even though going to university to become a journalist had been a lifelong dream, being with my family was equally important. I thought it would help if I slept on it after the New Year.

Since the apartment was such a quiet place, I thought it might improve our relationship to bring some light into the darkness so I bought a CD player.

Through Duane, I learned to rock with Bon Jovi, hum with Aerosmith, and air guitar with Led Zeppelin. I bought a few Bon Jovi t-shirts and saw them in concert, rocking out to *Rock of Love*.

While I rocked with Bon Jovi, my brother on the other hand, had passion for Khanh Ly, a famous Vietnamese singer. He ate rice while I enjoyed french fries. I spoke English while he spoke Vietnamese. I had many friends, while he had many empty beer cans. I enjoyed playing hockey, he enjoyed watching TV. And while I enjoyed camping in the summer, my brother enjoyed complaining, and was and getting grumpier.

I was consistently excelling at school but my brother was constantly looking for a job. Ever since that fateful day, in which we learned of the requirements of family sponsorship, Tan had become somber. He began to drink even more heavily and was fired for drinking on the job. On many nights he stumbled home from a day searching for work, drunk and swearing about his problems. In slurred broken English, he blamed people for not understanding him, cursed the weather for being so cold, attacked the bus system for not being on time and condemned life for being unfair.

The differences between us eventually took a turn for the worse one cold November evening. When I arrived home from a hockey game around midnight, I saw Tan lying in the hallway of our apartment. He had been too drunk to open the door. I helped him up and sat him on the sofa. He was barely conscious but regardless, I decided to confront him about his drinking problem.

As I spoke to him he grew more and more irate and defensive. He began to treat me like he had back home. I was the little brother, with no right to criticize him. I plowed on, telling him that he should stop drinking or it would hurt him in the long run. He didn't listen. He only got angrier as I continued disgracing him.

I thought that at eighteen I was an adult, and I wanted to help him. We were brothers, and in my eyes, I was right for telling him to stop drinking because I cared for him. Yet, as I sat expressing my concerns, he slowly got up, stared me down and slapped me across the face. Surprised and shocked, I tumbled to the floor. He started to yell at me, calling me horrible names. I tried to stand but stars circled my head. A punch came out of nowhere and hit my cheek, sending me sprawling into the table. Cups tumbled to the floor, shattering into pieces. My cheek felt like someone had put a hot iron on my face. Trembling, I touched my face with my fingers, but I couldn't feel it. I yelled at Brother, asking what he was doing.

"I am teaching you a lesson, young brother," he said, grabbing hold of me. He was so close I could smell the alcohol on his breath. His bloodshot eyes glared at me. "At home, I am your older brother. I rule the house! As a younger brother, all you do is obey."

He was about to slap me again, but I blocked it. I pushed him away and he stumbled back a few feet. “We are in Canada. We are not back home.” I stood defiantly and shouted, “We are no longer Vietnamese. When we chose to leave our country and immigrate here, we gave up our identity. We are Canadian now. You should learn to live like one!” I spoke to him with such contempt that I could see in his eyes he was ready to kill me. He looked like a tiger that had been poked and harassed, that had had enough of the little lamb making fun of it.

He came at me with ferocity and anger, grabbing hold of my shirt. He threw me against the wall. I wanted to fight back, to kick and to punch until the last man was standing, but Father had taught me better.

“You think your education, your shopping malls, and your English will wash your yellow skin away and make you like those other Canadians? Give me a break! You are a root-forgetter!” He pointed a finger in my face, screaming.

I tried to push him away, but his hand was around my neck, and he was squeezing it. I couldn't breathe. He was tightening his grip. I gasped for air and my eyes began to pop. I fought to get loose, but he was overpowering me. I felt weak. With a last breath, I called his name, "Anh Tan." He realized then that he was about to kill me and eased off. I grabbed the opportunity and pushed him away.

I rushed for the door and shouted back at him, “I am a grown man now. I can choose to live how I want.” I ran down the street and kept on running until I could run no longer. His voice echoed in my head. “Root-forgetter.” Had I forgotten who I was? I am a Canadian now, I told myself. The day that I stepped onto that boat was the day I had accepted Canada as my country. I was no longer

Vietnamese. I had to move on. Tan, however, still held fast to whatever was left of the Vietnamese in him. I walked until I was able to put what had just happened into a container and then I did with it what I did with every other conflict—sealed it and buried it away.

Anger dissipated and I decided to go home. Upon entering our apartment, I saw my brother curled up on the sofa, dozing off. I walked past him and into the bedroom. The acceptance letter to the University of Saskatchewan was lying on my bed. I unfolded it and read it again.

Few days after the incident, I returned to our apartment to find him having a beer with a friend. They were laughing about something, but as I entered the room they stopped. Tan called out my name and lurched towards me, putting his arm around my neck. I could clearly smell his beer stench. His eyes were red, and he seemed high. His hands were shaking and his pupils were dilated.

Lucy introduced herself. She had a smell that seemed like she hadn't taken a bath for a long time and her teeth were rotten and black. I turned to Tan and asked him why he was home so early. He responded that he had found a job that morning but his stupid boss had fired him that afternoon. He defended himself saying it was just a bottle of Hennessey and the boss had plenty in his cabinet. I didn't want any more trouble, so I went to my room.

Without a job, Tan had even more time to get liquored up, and with a companion he had even more encouragement to do it. Things escalated to a point where I even caught him snorting heroin in our bathroom. He no longer wanted to look for a job; he was no longer interested in life. He just wanted to lose himself and shut out the world. I wanted to talk to him and help him but every time I tried, he was either too high or too drunk to carry on a conversation.

Returning home from a hockey game one night I found the place a mess, like someone had torn it apart. Clothes were scattered all over, and books and papers lay in a pile of garbage. I rushed over to the drawer where I kept Mother's necklace, the only keepsake that reminded me of her. It was gone. I went through the apartment and saw no sign of forced entry, and Tan wasn't home.

About half an hour later, he arrived with a case of beer and Lucy. His eyes were bloodshot and he seemed hyper. I confronted him about the necklace. He didn't even bother to look at me. He just went to the sofa, turned on the TV and pretended I wasn't there.

"Where is my necklace?" I persisted. I stood in front of him and the TV, pointed my finger in his face, and demanded to know what he had done with it. His body language was cold and heavy. I began accusing him, but he did nothing more than ask me to move away from the TV. I held my position in rebellion. He told me to move or else he was going to show me who was boss. I demanded to know why he would take the only thing that helped me remember Mother. Before I could finish the sentence, a hard kick to my stomach threw me against the wall, next to the TV stand. As I lay there trying to catch my breath, Tan loudly said, “This is my house and my rules. If you don’t like it, leave.”

He sat back on the sofa, where Lucy joined him with a beer. I lay gasping for air next to the TV for ten minutes before I could muster enough energy to move. I went to the bedroom and packed all my belongings into a black garbage bag and hauled it to the street. As I left the apartment, I could hear his voice follow me out the door. "When you leave, don't ever come back."

I called Duane, who had already moved to Saskatoon and had rented an apartment. He had asked me to join him, but I had been hesitant because of Tan, we only had each other as family. Now, the anger boiled inside me and nudged me into action. Why had he forgotten all of the teachings of our parents? My necklace had been a memento from Mother. "Why would you take that away?" I shouted into the darkness. Mother hadn't raised her children to be thieves or barbarians. I condemned Brother while I waited for the bus to arrive. Angry as I was with Tan, by the time the bus came I already missed him. Rain soaked my face as I stood outside the Greyhound bus terminal.

I never imagined that fight would be the last time I saw Tan. Our goodbye should never have been in such a manner. We had struggled through so much together, and our relationship had started out so strong. I felt a deep sense of loss when I looked back and contemplated what had gone so wrong. Luckily, I found a woman who would eventually help me to understand myself and my lost relationship with Brother.

Chapter 16

Tây Sơn Dynasty

In 1771, the Tây Sơn revolution broke out in Quy Nhơn, which was under the control of the Nguyễn. The leaders of this revolution were three brothers named Nguyễn Nhạc, Nguyễn Lữ, and Nguyễn Huệ, not related to the Nguyễn lords.

After arriving in Saskatoon, I got a job as a delivery driver for *Hot 2 for 1 Pizza.* Every night after class I would work until two in the morning, then rush home to squeeze in a few hours of sleep before getting up for my morning classes. It was tiring, but it provided a means to support myself and it was a fun job. I had many interesting run-ins with customers. One man wanted to trade pizza for marijuana and one girl who was hungry and didn't have any money wanted to sleep with me in return for the pizza. I gave it to her instead and paid the boss from my pocket.

The owner of *Hot 2 for 1 Pizza* was Tony, a short round Italian with a mustache that made him look like Mario from the *Super Mario* game. When I had first come looking for a job, he scanned me up and down as though he had had an infrared camera. Wordlessly he patted me on back and said I was hired. The funniest thing about Tony was that he spoke more with his hands than with words. When he needed to express himself, it was like watching a puppeteer in action: hands and fingers pointing in all directions.

When I started the job, I was slow. *Hot 2 For 1* promised delivery to your door within an hour or the pizza was free. Finding many of the addresses in a new city was tough. When we were busy, I had to carry two or three pizzas in the car. I'd rush to one address but if it took a long time to find then finding the second and third would stretch that one-hour even more. As a result, some of the pizzas were free. I came back crushed, worried about losing my job. Tony cried foul for missing the deliveries, pulling his hair when things didn't go too well, but in the end he decided to keep me around and told me, "Now you know where that customer lives so you can get there faster next time. I have many loyal customers." He encouraged me to keep on learning instead of berating or firing me for missing a delivery. True to his word, many of the same customers called every week for a pizza and those same customers had kept Tony in business for the past twenty-three years.

Delivering pizza for Tony, I learned to navigate around Saskatoon extremely well. There was one lesson, however, that taught me that nothing is more valuable than life. This I would never forget thanks to a scar on the right side of my throat.

It happened a few days before Christmas. The snow was brutal. Forecasts expected it to accumulate to two feet. The wind blew mercilessly and cut through to the bone, and it was non-stop. Because of the weather the pizza shop was busy. It was only ten o'clock and I had delivered more than fifty pizzas, twice as many as on a regular day.

My yellow, beat-up Honda Civic crawled slowly to each stop. Around one in the morning when things had quieted down a little, a call came in for a delivery on the west side of the Saskatchewan River. I had been there before, it was a run-down housing complex infested with gangs and drugs. But I had had no problems there until that evening.

I found the building number, parked the car and went out to look for the unit. Most people were already cozied up in their beds, and so the place was dark and quiet. I passed through an alleyway on my way to unit 27. As I came around the dark corner, a hand grabbed me from behind and a cold sharp blade pressed on my throat. The voice told me to drop the pizza, which I did immediately. Then it asked for my wallet.

Worried about making my rent for the month, I decided to try negotiating with the perpetrator. I pleaded with him and begged him to leave my wallet, telling him I needed the money for school and housing. Without it, I would be living on the street. I asked the crook to just take the pizza. "Shut up or else," the voice said. I could feel the anger shake through his vocal chords, and the smell of marijuana violated my nose.

Before I could utter another word, a sharp pain shot through the right side of my neck. I fell face down to the ground and screamed at the top of my lungs for help. I held my left hand to my neck and saw blood ooze through my fingers, painting the snow crimson. The attacker frisked my body looking for the wallet. Trying to save the few dollars I had, I rolled away, screaming "Murder!" for attention. Dogs began to bark and lights turned on. A woman shouted from across the street and I picked myself up and ran toward her.

Blood dripped from the wound down to my elbow. I turned to check on my attacker, but no one was behind me; there was only a trail of blood. I got to the door and the woman let me in and called the cops.

Minutes later, an army of police cruisers descended on the housing complex while a helicopter and canines woke the whole neighborhood from their slumber.

The ambulance took me to the emergency room where a doctor put six stitches in my neck, telling me that had it been an inch closer to the artery I would have been dead. I called Tony, told him about the incident and apologized about the pizza, expecting him to throw a tantrum. Instead, he came to the hospital and drove me home.

When I got back to my apartment Duane was more dramatic. He treated me like I was some helpless person. He got me drinks. When I complained that I was cold, he got me blankets. He changed the channel when I watched TV. He even did my homework. He and Tony took turns lecturing me for being stupid, telling me that I could have died and that protecting my money wasn't worth my life.

I went to bed and thought about it. They were right. I could have died, had not some greater power been looking out for me. I should have given my wallet to the attacker and worked harder to pay rent but I hadn't and it had almost gotten me killed.

Few days after the incident I went back to work. Tony was happy to see me. He was getting worried and with the little help he had, I was his lifesaver. Concerned for my safety, Tony gave me a little device about the size of my palm with a number pad and an earpiece. I asked him what it was and he told me it was a cellular phone. I thanked Tony for looking out for me. He said I was like his family, and if I ever needed anything, all I had to do was ask.

It had been two years since I moved to Saskatoon and I longed for a family. I missed Brother terribly. There were many times when I wanted to call him and check in on him, but I kept thinking back to that terrible night. I was still angry and stopped myself from taking such foolish actions. I studied and worked harder to occupy my mind.

Over the years that I delivered pizza, there was one order that I looked forward to every Friday. It was an order for the building next to mine, and it was the same every time: small vegetarian with extra olives. The money was always in an envelope when I got there. All I had to do was leave the pizza at the door. In the envelope there was money and an elegantly written note, thanking me and wishing me a good night.

I was fascinated by this mysterious customer and wanted to find out who it was and why I never had the chance to see him or her. Feeling lucky to be alive after the robbery, I told myself that I would find out who this person was. The next time the order came in I worked out a plan. I drove to the apartment and parked the car instead of leaving it running. I looked at the window of the unit and saw that the lights were on. Someone must be home, I thought.

I went up the stairs to the door and, sure enough, the envelope was waiting for me. Instead of just dropping the pizza and leaving though, I knocked. A minute went by with no answer, so I knocked a second time, a bit louder. I waited another five minutes. I thought it odd for a light to be on inside the apartment if no one was home.

As I was about to leave, I heard footsteps. The door opened and there stood a young woman in a bathrobe, white as an angel. She was petite with blond hair and freckles on her thin nose. I couldn't help but stare into her deep green eyes. It felt like time had stopped. Birds started to chirp and I could swear I heard Lionel Richie sing, *Hello? Is it me you're looking for?*

We stood there with our eyes locked for well over a minute without moving or making a sound, lost in Cupid's world. I felt like the soul had been sucked out of me and Medusa had turned me into a human statue.

The spell was broken by the footsteps of a man next door. I handed her the pizza and she quickly closed the door. I wanted to say something to her. I wanted to at least ask her name, but my mouth simply said "thank you." I heard a hushed "You're welcome," from the other side of the door.

I walked to my car cursing myself. *Thank you?* That was all I could come up with? I saw the most beautiful girl in the world and all I said was thank you? I wondered what was wrong with me.

I continued to analyze and condemn my stupidity on the drive back to the shop. A picture of the green-eyed Medusa flashed constantly across my windshield. At the shop I paced back and forth like a zombie, talking to myself. Tony thought I was in trouble again.

He laughed and made fun of me when I told him about what had happened with the beautiful Medusa. He encouraged me to call and ask her out. He told me how suave he had been with his wife, Lindsay. The first time they met at an Italian café, he brought her flowers. The next day he brought her a necklace. They went out a few times, and within three months, he had proposed to her. Thanks to an unexpected pregnancy they got married quickly thereafter. After twenty-five years of marriage, they had two beautiful daughters and a son.

Tony was like a father to me. He loved me and cared for me as he did his own son. When the nights were slow, he paid me a little extra. He asked about my life and about my family. My story reminded him of his own immigration to Canada with his uncle. He told me that it was lonely for him at first and the Canadian winters were particularly harsh and cruel. In the beginning, Tony had started working at an Italian restaurant downtown as a busboy. He had worked very hard and within three months was promoted to waiter but he hated it. He said that it was the only job in the world where you're given food but you can't eat it.

He labored at a job he hated for ten years and saved enough money to open a pizza store. He always liked to make pizza, he told me. His mother had passed on her passion when he was still a child and it was a passion he took with him into adulthood. He wanted to share with the world the wonderful food his mother made for him at home in Italy.

Tony often invited me to his home, including every Thanksgiving and Christmas. He understood I didn't have a family and would be by myself during the holidays. At Tony's, everyone gathered around a table full of turkey, ham, mashed potatoes and many other delicacies. They all shared and laughed and told stories. I wanted to have a big family like Tony's.

I loved every moment I spent at his house. I yearned for the day when I would have someone to share those experiences with, but I knew I wasn't ready. I didn't have a career to support someone I loved. I didn't have much money in the bank. How could I start a family with so little to my name?

Every time I left Tony's house, I would wander through my apartment thinking about life, and conclude that education was more important at this point in my life than anything else. But once the image of Medusa entered my mind, it wouldn't leave - her glittering eyes, her pink lips. Her soft voice echoed in my head, like an angel whispering in my ear.

I would have gone insane from the spell of Medusa if it hadn't been for Duane. Since moving to Saskatoon, he had become an even better friend. He loaned me some money to get by before I could find a job. In the beginning, he even helped me buy groceries. In return for his help, I kept the place neat and clean.

Unlike me, Duane didn't have any problem with girls. Being Canadian and outgoing, he found dating easy. Occasionally I grew jealous of his skills with women, but there was really no comparison between us—he was six foot two compared to my meager five foot eight; he was talkative and smooth whereas I was shy and conservative. The only thing I had going for me was my money-smile, with straight teeth and a dimple. But it carried me only so far and usually only received a reciprocating smile.

When I told Duane about my Medusa in the next building, he wanted to go over and knock on her door immediately. He would have done if I hadn't pulled him back. I wanted to do it on my terms. Every day, Duane would ask about my dream girl and then go on to dispense some of his advices and secrets about women.

A week can go by very slowly when you want it to go fast. I was looking forward to delivering that pizza to Medusa. When Friday came around, I looked at my watch every five minutes, waiting, agonizing, as time slowly went on. But like many times in life, when you desperately want something to happen, it rarely does. Her call never came through.

I went home that evening feeling defeated, wondering when I would have a chance to talk to her again. I promised myself that if I ever did, I would try to get to know her.

As I got out of my car and began walking toward my building, I saw a green Volkswagen Beetle drive past me. I saw Medusa in the driver's seat, her soft pink lips pressed together in a smile. She waved at me, and I stood there frozen in her gaze. I let her eyes put a spell on me, willingly.

Chapter 17

Nguyễn Dynasty & French protectorate (1802 – 1945)

In 1784, during the conflict between Nguyễn Ánh, the surviving heir of the Nguyễn Lords, and the Tây Sơn Dynasty, a French Catholic Bishop, Pigneaux de Behaine, sailed to France to seek military backing for Nguyễn Ánh. At Louis XVI's court, Pigneaux brokered the Little Treaty of Versailles which promised French military aid in return for Vietnamese concessions.

Another week rolled by even more slowly. I counted the days until I might see her again. My mind was under her spell and there was no way to escape. During lectures I idly drew her picture, scribbled her name and dreamed of things to say to her once I met her again. I tried hard to break the spell by focusing on my education.

Studying to be a journalist for the past three years was fairly easy at the University of Saskatchewan. I liked most of the classes, but the one I took particular interest in and looked forward to every week was *Critical Thinking*, a fantastic class put on by the philosophy department. It was taught by Mr. Nufis, a mature Bangladeshi with dark trimmed hair, a full beard and stained-yellow teeth from heavy smoking; he had bulging eyes, and years of physical training had given him a sturdy body that commanded respect.

He taught the class in a very interesting manner, speaking with a wealth of knowledge to help bring his students into the world of thinking. He encouraged us to seek knowledge, for knowledge is the truth and to seek the truth is to find life worth living. His favorite quote was from the cave analogy in Plato's Republic, "Only knowledge can free you from the chains of illusion."

During Mr. Nufis' lessons, he spoke non-stop in his heavy English accent, never breaking to allow anyone to ask questions. I felt he was a glass full of knowledge and I was eager to drink it.

An assignment was handed out at the beginning of each session, typically on a relatively mundane topic such as "What are your thoughts on a chicken?" It was a one-sentence question and he expected a full-page essay. If you returned with a one-sentence answer, like many first year students, you would get an F.

He made the point at the beginning of every new semester that this was a critical thinking class and all answers needed to reflect that. For instance, when he asked us to consider a cow, we might consider it from the standpoint that to many, it's an animal, to others it's food, and to some it's a religious symbol. Why would an object like a cow have so much meaning? He wanted us to question even our own answers so we could learn to defend them with well thought out evidence. It was a systematic approach which I liked very much because, being a future journalist, I knew I would need to prove to my readers that I had carefully researched and thought about my subject.

Under his tough exterior, Mr. Nufis was a very nice person. This was proven on one occasion when I caught the flu and had to stay in bed for a week. I had a runny nose, eyes so watery I could barely see, and was constantly sneezing. To avoid spreading this to anyone else, I stayed home. I asked Duane to give Mr. Nufis a note for me, afraid I might have to retake the final exam that was fast approaching.

I found Mr. Nufis at my apartment door that very same day. He said that since I was too sick to go to class, the class would come to me. He brought a tape recorder so that if I was too tired and started to doze off, I could finish listening to his lecture afterward. If not for getting sick, I wouldn't have found out what a likeable person Mr. Nufis was. He took the time to come to my apartment throughout the week to give me the luxury of a one-on-one education.

After finishing his lectures, Mr. Nufis and I had many delightful conversations over tea. I got a chance to learn about his wife, Margaret. They had been married for forty years but never had any children. He wanted them very much, but he told me that God had a reason for not giving him the precious angels he surely deserved. He concluded that God had given him many young minds to educate, teach and guide. God had given him more than just one child; he had given him a class full of them. That was why he taught with such rigor, because he wanted to give all his knowledge to his children.

He told me he was getting older and didn't feel he had much time left, which was why he didn't stop for questions in class. Besides, he further explained, all questions could be answered if we would just look. If we had the patience, we could find all the answers to any question. I hoped he was right—especially about the question related to the feelings I had for Medusa.

When the weekend rolled around I couldn't help thinking about her. I told myself many times to go over and simply say "hi," and get to know her, but I never had the courage to do it. Duane made fun of me and offered to do it on my behalf. I refused.

I didn't even know who she really was as a person. Her personality could have been totally different from mine and we might argue day and night. Even worse, she could be a crazy person, who would haunt me for the rest of my life. But it didn't matter how I tried to argue myself out of her: my heart always begged to differ. It beat a little faster every time I thought about her. It raced even faster every time I parked the car at my building and looked over, hoping to catch a glimpse of her.

I wasn't able to concentrate at all. Every waking moment was a moment of her. I daydreamed of how to talk to her and what I would say. I almost died a few time due to not looking where I was going, but in the end nothing mattered but the image of Medusa, she who had bewitched me.

Lionel Ritchie became my friend. *Hello?* occupied every spare moment. I sang every word and replayed the song every day in my room. Even Duane started to pick up the phone and sing into it, just to make fun of me.

At the library, I perused many books about women such as *Men are from Mars, Women are from Venus,* hoping to find answers to my dilemma. I found some tips such as women like men who are confident. But the many books I found dealing with women's emotions and their biology didn't help me overcome the roadblock of talking to Medusa. Instead it just embarrassed me. A guy should not know more about a woman's physical makeup than she does. After a full day at the library without any real answers, I settled in to watch *Titanic* because from what Duane told me, many of his girlfriends liked this kind of movie.

Living with Duane was like living with my polar opposite. He was a bit of a womanizer and he liked to party. I found it fascinating that he had so much energy. He partied all night and never required a wink of sleep. Several times he asked me to come along to some of his frat parties, which I hesitantly did. But the blaring music hurt my ears, and drinking, pot smoking and stinking vomit really weren't my things. Duane seemed at home in it, though. That's where he seemed to belong.

The best thing about Duane was that he had a knack for starting conversation. He could talk on the phone with girls all night long. He had an inability to hear himself speak, therefore his volume tended to be pretty loud even in a normal conversation. On the other hand, I was reserved, quiet, and a bit shy. Our personalities could not have been more different, yet somehow we got along very well.

The funniest thing about Duane was that even though he was grown up, he could be easily scared. There was one incident just after moving into the apartment when I was in my bedroom studying. All of a sudden, I heard a really loud scream. It sounded like a girl screaming bloody murder from our bathroom. Immediately, I got up and charged in to investigate, only to find Duane half-naked, standing on the toilet and pointing at a cockroach. It became our little secret. Every time he teased me about being too scared to go talk to Medusa, I would threaten him with the story of the cockroach. Living with Duane was fun, and we were the best of buddies.

After having enough of his teasing and enough of *Titanic*, I went out and bought a dozen roses. I also bought a blank card and wrote, "I hope you like them," with the pizza shop number at the bottom, and signed it "The Pizza Guy." I delivered her pizza along with the roses that Friday night at eight when the call came through. I rushed back to the shop, hoping to get a response. It was a slow night and I waited for what seemed like an eternity for the call. I picked up the phone a few times to make sure there was still a dial tone. Could the flowers have been stolen? I convinced myself that she must not have received them because some idiot next door had snatched them, and I reasoned that I should call and tell her myself what had happened. I was beyond antsy and made up all sorts of excuses why I hadn't received at least a phone call in thanks.

I paced back and forth in front of the pizza oven, talking to myself. I told myself some jackass must have grabbed the dozen, fresh red roses and given them to his girlfriend, and was now thanking a stupid guy like me for leaving them unattended. Maybe she had a boyfriend, I thought to myself. "Great, Manny, you fell for a girl with a boyfriend. Of all the girls, you had to end up liking a girl who was maybe even already married. That's why she didn't call," I thought to myself.

As the night went on, the list of reasons for not receiving a call got longer. About ten minutes to midnight, the phone rang and I answered, thinking it was an order for pizza. The line was quiet. I looked at the call display to see that it read Jenny Newton. It was my Medusa. She said in her soft voice, "Thank you for the flowers." My heart sprinted a mile a minute and I grinned widely, happy as a bird taking flight for the first time. I stood there holding the telephone as though my life depended on it. I asked Jenny if it would be all right to call her sometime for a coffee or maybe even for dinner. I promised her it wouldn't be pizza. She laughed out loud and said I was funny.

When I hung up, Tony looked over at me and noticed my grin. He patted me on the back and gave me the keys, telling me to lock the door at closing because he was going home to be with his wife. That night I barely slept.

A few days later I took Jenny out for dinner to a fancy restaurant on Second Avenue. I felt like I was the luckiest guy in the world, as I saw her in her blue dress, with her curly hair and her green eyes, standing in front of her apartment waiting for me. During the evening, I gave her my undivided attention. I wanted to know everything about her.

She was pretty shy. Every time we locked eyes, she would be too timid to look at me for longer than a second or two. After some food, we felt more comfortable and I asked her about her life and her school. She said she was from a small town called Paradise Hill, about a three-hour drive from the university. She was from a family of very dedicated Christians, which explained why she didn't want to drink. She was an only child, her dad was a church pastor and her mom was a teacher at the local elementary school. Growing up, she had the full attention of her mom and dad. Because of a complication, her mother never had another child and Jenny missed out on having someone to talk with and listen to.

Jenny was in her third year at the university, same as me. She wanted to be a psychologist and so was majoring in psychology. I jokingly asked her whether our date would be just another case study for her. She cheerfully said that it wouldn't be a date at all then.

While at university, Jenny was also working at the Midtown Plaza as a part-time cashier. She liked the job.

The money was enough to pay for her day-to-day expenses and her co-workers were easy to get along with. She didn't like the store manager, however, because he had asked her out a few times and despite her having told him she was not interested, he persisted. She said she was afraid that he might harm her. After listening to her concerns, I told her that I could be her bodyguard if she would let me. She answered, "We'll see" and smiled.

As the night went on, I learned that we shared the same teacher, Mr. Nufis. We both laughed every time our professor and his unique personality came up. Jenny was surprised when I told her Mr. Nufis was a good friend of mine and that he often came to my apartment to chat. She wanted to meet him, which I agreed to arrange if she agreed to go on a second date with me. Upon hearing that, she told me with a smirk that I must have lots of girlfriends because I was so smooth.

I took this comment to mean she wanted to know my dating history. I confessed to her that I had never had a girlfriend and that I didn't believe in dating around. I wanted to invest time on only one person whom I truly loved, and I didn't believe in sleeping with anyone besides my wife. I told her that was how I was taught and raised. She laughed and called me old-fashioned but added that she liked that in a man. She reached out and placed her hand in mine, making sure that I had caught her meaning. The warmth of her hand zipped through my body, touched my heart, and I could feel my heart zing with excitement.

My heart began pounding like an elephant stampede. It beat at 100 miles an hour like thousands of mammoths heading south in single file. I felt lucky at that moment that the doctors had repaired my heart because I surely would have died from a heart attack if they hadn't.

Time passes quickly when love is in the air. It was getting close to midnight and Jenny told me she had to be home as she had promised her mother she wouldn't stay out after midnight. That was the only stipulation from her family when she had moved out to live on campus.

I drove Jenny back to her apartment and walked her to her door. I didn't know whether to kiss her or not. I stood there watching the scene unfold, debating in my head. Should I? Looking into her eyes I could see she was struggling with the same question. In the end, we both held onto that little secret and parted for the night.

Walking back to the car, the night was cold, but I felt warm all over. In the apartment, Duane woke to the sound of my arrival. He settled on the couch and with a grin began to grill me for details. I told him my mother had taught me never to kiss and tell, so I went to my room and cheerfully went to sleep, dreaming of the day I would see Jenny again.

After a few of months of casual dating, we began to see each other on a regular basis. We kept in contact daily, talking for hours on the phone. Duane asked me whether I was sleeping with her, but Jenny and I both agreed that sex should happen only after we were married, as we had talked about at the beginning of our relationship.

Jenny told me that before our relationship could go any further, her parents had to provide their approval. She trusted her parents very much and felt they should give their blessing for our relationship. If for some reason they disapproved of me that would be the end of it. She told me this up front so we didn't have to hurt each other in the long run.

I prepared for our meeting much the way I would prepare for a job interview. I rehearsed in front of the mirror. I paced back and forth pretending to shake hands with Jenny's father. I read *How To Ace a Job Interview.* I sat straight and I spoke slowly and clearly, providing examples of qualifications and experiences.

When I asked Duane to role-play, he thought it was for an actual job interview and thus treated it like one. He spoke like an employer while I acted as a prospective candidate, sweating and nervous. When he learned I was really preparing to meet Jenny's family, he burst out laughing at me. Then he pretended to be an old man, asking me what I wanted to do with his daughter. "Was I a pervert who would break his young girl's heart?" I wasn't laughing and I answered honestly about my feelings for Jenny. I loved her very much.

The role-playing wasn't helpful at all when I met Jenny's parents. I dressed in a black suit with a gray shirt and blue tie, and we drove to her house for Thanksgiving weekend. When I stepped into the house, I was so nervous sweat ran down my cheeks. Mr. Newton, seeing me sweating so much, thought I might have a heart attack. They were also surprised I was in a suit. Mr. and Mrs. Newton settled me down and offered me tea and biscuits. Jenny and her mother excused themselves to the kitchen to prepare dinner while Mr. Newton and I chatted.

Mr. Newton was a nice man in his fifties, easy going with gray hair and dark glasses that made him look more like an English professor than a pastor. We started off talking about school. He asked me what I wanted to do and I told him I wanted to be a journalist. "Journalism is an honest and dignified profession," Mr. Newton said. He told me that he rarely saw kids these days study journalism as most wanted to be the next Bill Gates or

Steve Jobs. In my mind, I scored a point and was praying for more.

At the dinner table while saying grace, Jenny grinned at me and in a quiet voice told me her mother thought I was cute and was fond of my politeness. Two points, I thought. A few more and I might eventually get the job.

During dinner, Mrs. Newton asked about my family. I hesitated. After few moments, I gathered myself and told them about Vietnam, my lovely farmer parents and my harrowing escape on a small fishing boat. I shared with them the struggles and triumphs in the refugee camps and the loneliness of coming to Canada. I reminisced about Mother, how I longed to see her again and how I missed my brother and sister.

When Jenny and I left to drive back to Saskatoon on Sunday afternoon, Mr. and Mrs. Newton asked that I look after their only child. Feeling happy and honored that they had entrusted me with such a valuable part of their lives, I reminded myself never to throw that trust away.

Standing at Jenny's apartment, a kiss lingered in our minds again. And so while hugging goodbye, our faces touched and our lips found each other's. The world was a bed of tulip covered in rainbows. I could feel the heat rush to her head and her face turned red. Without even a goodbye, Jenny rushed inside and shut the door.

Intoxicated by love, life became full of roses and songs by Lionel Richie. When I got home Duane saw my beaming face and asked what had happened. I didn't respond, instead headed to my bedroom. He understood and stuck his tongue out to demonstrate how I should have done it. He looked like a cow licking a rock.

Lying in bed, I was unable to sleep. After meeting Jenny's parents, I missed Brother tremendously. I felt so alone, even though I was about to realize my dream of becoming like Tintin, and I was in love with a beautiful girl. My future looked bright and shiny, but I couldn't help thinking about Tan. I wondered how he was doing. Did he miss me? I missed him terribly. Concerned about opening the sealed box that haunted me, I persuaded my mind to go to sleep and, like a trained animal, it did.

Chapter 18

After Nguyễn Ánh established the Nguyễn Dynasty in 1802, he tolerated Catholicism and employed some Europeans in his court as advisors. However, he and his successors were conservative Confucians who resisted Westernization.

In a flash, five years had passed since I started down the road toward becoming my childhood hero. Graduation was fast approaching, and, thanks to Mr. Nufis' connections, I had a job lined up with the *Saskatoon Star Phoenix*. The position was as a writer for the human interest section. I was excited about it and knew I would do a good job after volunteering at *The Sheaf*, the university newspaper.

Putting thoughts into words and communicating them with other people was such a rewarding experience. The written word had evolved to teach and to maintain a wealth of understanding about the universe around us. To participate in this process was a dream come true for me, and Tan had played a big part in that journey.

I tried many times without success to call Brother to join me for my graduation. It had been five years since we had last seen each other. We had spoken only a handful of times and every time he was too drunk or too high to have a meaningful conversation with me. I left messages with Lucy to ask him to call, but he never did.

On graduation day, I hoped he would just show up. I stood on the stage to accept the honor. I looked into the crowd and wished he was there among the many other families cheering for me, applauding me for all the sacrifices we made on this journey to realize my dream. But he never showed up.

I had many friends come to congratulate me, but I really just wanted Tan there. No one else really mattered. Jenny put a few good words in for Brother and told me that perhaps he was busy with a new job. I took those words to heart and told myself the same and moved on. I celebrated the biggest day of my life, a victory 23 years in the making, without any family members. I felt I had won the battle but lost the war.

I graduated at the top of my class on June 28, 2003, five years after I had left Brother behind. Many honors were bestowed on me, including *the person most likely to succeed* in our yearbook.

Later that evening, as I was getting ready to go out to celebrate, a call came in. I was busy putting on my clothes so Duane answered it. He rushed into my room with a grave look on his face and handed me the phone. Lucy was on the other end. She told me that my brother had been admitted into the hospital for a drug overdose. She'd found him on his bed that afternoon with no vital signs.

I dropped the phone. My knees felt weak and I fell to the floor. Duane quickly came to my aid and held the phone to my ear. Without hesitation, I took the car and headed for Royal Alexandra hospital in Medicine Hat.

On the way, memories of Brother rushed back to

me. The struggles he had had back home, the delay in our immigration process, the tears we shared together in Bidong as we longed for our family and the emptiness and sadness we had when we learned we couldn't sponsor our family. Those memories shone as brightly as the headlights of my car, which penetrated the darkness for the seven-hour journey to the hospital. I reached the hospital just before 3 a.m., only to be told to prepare for his funeral.

Seeing him lying there at the morgue, I wept. The years had changed him. He had aged considerably. He was extremely thin, he had grown a beard, and his hair was uncut.

The needle marks were clearly visible on his left arm. Why, I thought, would someone want to do that with their life? And why leave me all alone in this world? We were brothers.

I felt so hollow inside. We hadn't even had a chance to say goodbye. I wanted to speak to him again, to have just a little more time with him. I didn't care about my university education or being a journalist any more. None of that was important at that moment. I was such a selfish bastard; I could only see what was in front of my eyes. I blamed myself. "I am sorry, Brother, I had forgotten about you. I am a root-forgetter. I have been so obsessed with this western culture that I have forgotten who I am." I didn't get to say goodbye, but I did see Tan's body before he turned to ash.

I went by his apartment to get some of his belongings. Lucy handed me a letter that she found in his room. The letter was in his illegible handwriting and full of broken English.

Têt 2000, The year of the Dragon.

Dear Brother,

You are o.k. my little brother? The year of the Dragon is coming on us, me remember this year, you now 21 years old. We live here, in Canada for exactly 8 years. Me counted the number each days that we not home. Me miss mother very much and me wife too, and sister Mai. Me wanted to go home, but can't. Me don't like here. People look me funny when me walk down street. They look at me scare for me not white like them. Me want to eat rice with fish juice, and they don't here. Me good at farming brother; me don't know how to give people food. Me wish one day, me could be home back to our family. You, me know you liked it here. You have good future than old me. Me from a different world, a place that no cold, and neighbor come see you make sure you o.k. This world is not me. The more me hated this place, me find that stuff Lucy give me good.

More, its fill the hole in me of losing you. Me read the university's letter sent to you, me don't all understand it, but o.k. to know that your dream had come true. Me scare to lose you, but me don't want to hold you back behind. Me not as strong as mother, me love you so so much too much to see you go. When you left, me felt alone in darkness and the empty. Drinking with Lucy me feel better, no scare. No miss home and miss you. Me wish brother best, and wish brother find your way to ancestor.

Me love you long time,
Tan Tran

I tucked the letter in my wallet and kept it in the same chest that I had used for so many other memories I had buried away. I was afraid if I ever saw it again it might swallow me whole and destroy me. I was too weak to live with such painful memories. Like many things that went wrong in my life, I tucked it deep under that ocean, under layer upon layer of pain, hoping it would go away.

It did, but returned that fateful day when Mai was born, a year after Jenny and I got married. A flood of emotions engulfed me. The happy feeling of becoming a father coupled with the burden and responsibility of teaching my child. I began to question myself, "who am I?" Because all children are born with curiosity, they want to know their roots and ancestries.

Like a dam that had burst, the love, longing, and yearning swept me off my feet and carried me in search of an answer. Searching for the rich history and heritage that I had forgotten, I started finding ways to rediscover my roots. I was happy to learn Vietnam had joined the World Trade Organization in January 2007 and that the economic fortune of the country was beginning to change. Without knowing it, I subconsciously began planning a trip to discover myself. Then came the day when Mai asked me about my parents for the first time in her life. That was the final nudge that pushed me off the edge into the darkness of my past and into self-discovery.

Chapter 19

North & South (1945 – 1975)

The defeat of the Japanese by the Allies created a power vacuum for Vietnamese to seize power in August 1945 before French authorities were able to return to reclaim control of the government.

Long before the sun rises on the horizon, vendors start to open their stalls in Ho Chi Minh City. The fragrance of pho, the famous Vietnamese noodle soup, starts to permeate our hotel room. The noisy motorcycles and their riders navigate their way through the morning rays. The roosters begin to crow and people start their days, many at the coffee shop.

Unable to sleep and excited to greet my fellow Vietnamese, I wander across the street to the coffee shop near our hotel. The humming and yawning of the city can be heard loud and clear. The Vietnamese national anthem plays proudly on a speaker nearby.

I grab a plastic stool and sit down at a small table. The owner comes over, "Café?" he asks.

"Yes," I reply with a hint of broken Vietnamese in my vocal chords. He gives me a welcoming smile. I smile back in return, if only because you can't help but gravitate toward people with whom you share something in common in a foreign land, whether it is skin color, or physical resemblance.

I am mesmerized at being among the Vietnamese, the comrades I thought I would never see again. I feel happy and at peace just to sit in a corner cafe and peek into the lives of my people.

Startled by a tap on my shoulder, I turn to see a kid of about nine years old in a ragged t-shirt and shorts. He looks and smells like he hasn't taken a shower for three days. He smiles and puts out his hand to ask for money, and it reminds me of my days in Bidong begging for food. I take the wallet out of my back pocket and thumb through the bills of various values, sizes and colors.

In one swift movement, the kid snatches my wallet, turns the corner and disappears.

All of my identification is gone—credit cards, driver's license and even my family's spending money. I can't believe what has just happened. My own people have just mugged me in my own country.

I find my way to a police station about three blocks north of the hotel and speak with a young officer in a green uniform who looks too young to know anything about policing. He takes my name and my contact information and sends me on my way.

I am furious with Vietnam. The country is dirty, hot, and uncivilized. I am here to reclaim what is left of me, but instead I was humiliated by a Visa Officer and mugged by a nine-year-old. "Is this how the Vietnamese people welcome others?" I thought. If it is, I don't need to be here any longer. I walk back to the hotel, determined to pack up and head back to Canada and leave this god-forsaken place.

I stop in my tracks, however, when I get back to our room and see Mai sleeping. Her peaceful face lifts my anger and reminds me once again of the reason I am here. Coming back isn't solely for me to find out who I am, but for her sake. I am just tagging along, hoping to find some pieces of me that lie scattered in the dust of life.

When I tell Jenny what happened, I am angry, upset at myself, and embarrassed by my people. This is not how I want my people to behave, and this is not how I picture what my country has become. Jenny tries to comfort me by telling me she has some money, and goes on reminding me that at least I am safe and that the contents of my wallet can be replaced when we get back to Canada.

I feel miserable but decide go for a walk, hoping it will help me to feel better. Walking through the street, I can't help but wonders why the Vietnamese people seem like such savages. The kid has probably already gone through my wallet and has thrown it away in some trashcan. The more I think about it, the more upset I become.

After about thirty minutes of walking, I begin to feel thirsty. Checking my pocket for money, I find the business card from Nhan, the teacher I met at the airport. I borrow a phone from a vendor and call him. Nhan arrives at our hotel an hour later and I tell him what happened. He tells me that Ho Chi Minh City has become a dangerous place, but he asks that we don't let that one bad incident spoil our whole trip. I agreed, since Mai needs to know where she came from. She must find this out if she is to know where she'll be going in life. I should not color her quest with my opinions and feelings.

With no money left, Nhan offers to put us up at his home, and I accept.

Nhan has a nice family. His wife and two children are beautiful and kind. I am particularly fond of his wife, for she has the same voice and articulation as Mrs. Winona, my teacher in Bidong. Unable to control the floodgate that keeps leaking from inside me since my arrival, I confess to Nhan the purpose of this journey.

I stay up all night with Nhan, sharing my experiences. Early the next morning I depart with Jenny and Mai for Vinh Hanh in search of the life I once had.

Chapter 20

The history of Vietnam is one of the longest continuous histories in the world, with the oldest archaeological findings showing that people have been living there as far back as over a half million years ago.

I stand like a frozen statue. In front of me is a little hut with a coconut leaf roof and plastered mud walls. While Mai and Jenny stay outside, I go in to investigate. Pots and pans dangle near a bed made of multiple wooden planks that don't fit together. A blanket is neatly folded in half with a small pillow lying on top of it. Nestled in the back of the hut is an altar with two black and white pictures side by side. The photo on the left is of a young man. The photo on the right is of a woman with a dimple. There are two candles on each side of the altar and a big Buddhist inscription on the back wall.

"This is my house," I think to myself, "and those pictures are of Mother and Father." I rush to the altar and hold the pictures in my hands, and the smell of raisins envelops my whole being. Unable to move, a vision of my parents comes forward. They pat me on the head and I hug them. Holding both Mother and Father in my hands, I move to sit on the wooden bed. "This is our house," I announce to my parents. "I'm sorry I wasn't around to take care of you, Mother. I am such a bad child for neglecting you. I was so busy with material things that I abandoned you."

As I sit there feeling remorseful for my actions, a woman in a black Ba Ba, a southern Vietnamese traditional dress, walks in holding a rice pot. She wears a conical hat and mud covers most of her body. On seeing me, she looks up. Through her hat, I can see long lashes and hazel eyes. She drops the rice pot and rushes to wrap me in her arms. "Manh, is that you?" she asks in Vietnamese.

The voice sounds so familiar. I kneel down to have a closer look at the woman, at her hazel eyes, her curly hair, and her freckled face. Before I can answer she hugs me tighter, and calls my name like she did years earlier. Manh. The name echoes in my head, a comfortable name that has long been dormant but is now awoken by someone whose blood I share—my sister.

"You are home now, Brother. Manh, you are really home." She says this as though to confirm this is not a dream. Time has not been kind to her. She looks older than her years, the sun has made her darker, and she is thinner. I want to say that I miss her, I love her, and I have many stories to tell her, especially about Brother. I want to know about her life. I want to know what she's done all these years. I want to know about her living conditions, her jobs, and her family. I want to know everything that has happened. I want it so much, but my mouth is dry and the tears that have poured into my throat leave me gasping for air. My heartache paralyzes my frontal cortex and I can't do anything more than just hold her in my arms.

"Sister Mai, how are you?" It takes a concentrated effort for me to utter those words. I desire to say more, but flood of images from my mind have taken hold of me. The sealed box cracks open. The layers of walls smash. The iron chains break and a surge of emotions pour out with no way to stop them.

All the years of longing, sorrow, and loneliness come out of me and I cry like a baby. I curl up in the fetal position from all the terrors and fears that have been locked deep inside me. They enter my bloodstream like a virus and I shake and quiver. All the despair and misery that I have banished away, afraid they will kill me one day like Buon, are now released. A world of darkness and cold engulfs my heart. Grief and bitterness blanket my body, and I take in one last breath before saying goodbye to the evil world.

On the verge of the afterlife, a warm, radiant light surrounds my body. Soaked in the comfort of this light, I begin to regain control. Slowly, all the contagious viruses in my body begin to dissipate and leave me bathed in love. When I come to, my daughter, Jenny and Sister are beside me, all comforting me.

The four of us hold each other in deep embrace for over an hour. Abruptly, Sister stands up "you must be hungry," she announces, without waiting for a reply. She cleans up the shattered rice pot, grabs another, and begins dinner preparations.

We eat in dim candlelight as my family had done for many years. Sister and I recount some of the stories I told under this roof and the laughter that followed them. Even with my degree and well-paying job, I have never been truly happy until this night, eating dinner in this shabby hut with a mud floor and the people I love. I finally come to realize that it doesn't matter what I do. I will be satisfied just to live with the people I care for.

After dinner, Sister tells us what happened in the months after Tan and I left. Mother fell sick just a few weeks after we left. She developed a high fever and started hallucinating that Tan and I were still home. She had sold everything to pay for Brother and me to get to America, so there was no money to get medical assistance. She died three months later.

Before Mother was gone, she confessed to my sister that she didn't want me and Brother to leave, but she had to let us go. She hadn't wanted to destroy my dream. As a mother she would not have been able to face herself if she failed to help her child achieve his ultimate goal. Mother said she saw the future in me, and she wanted to give me an opportunity she never had.

I am very fortunate to have had a mother with love strong enough to send me into the world and inspire me to reach for my potential. It is only a Vietnamese mother who is strong, kind, and loving enough to do that and I forever admire her courage. Only the unequivocal love of a Vietnamese mother is able to understand that a future worth living is a future worth sacrificing.

Listening to Sister's experiences and learning she has lived alone since my mother died feels like a knife stab into my gut. I want to relive those moments when Mother died with her and help her get through them, but I know it will never happen. Time can never travel backward. Following this logic, Brother will never again see Sister, his wife, and his home.

Together with Sister and my family, we pay a visit to Loan, Tan's wife. I tell my sister-in-law what happened to Tan, of how he had longed for home and how he took up drinking and snorting heroin to cope with his loneliness. I can't help but blame myself for Brother's problems. If I had been there for him he wouldn't have died, and if I were stronger, I could have stopped it before it all started. But in the end Loan stops me. She tells me exactly what Tan had said earlier, "That's what brothers are for. Brothers are there to help you along the way and are willing to sacrifice anything to help you reach your goal."

These words help heal the wound that has lived inside me since Brother died.

We stay with Sister until it is time to leave Vietnam and head back to Canada. Jenny and Mai have grown fond of my sister, who insists they eat more to get fatter. She accuses me of being an awful father and a terrible husband for not feeding my wife and my child properly. It only gets worse when she learns I named my daughter after her.

The day before we're to leave, we go to visit the graves where my parents and our ancestors lie. I show Mai my father and mother. I tell her this is where her grandparents are sleeping and looking after us.

I show Jenny and Mai the green farmland that once belonged to our family and how it sits among field after field of paddies that provide so many Vietnamese livelihoods.

When the plane takes off and we leave Ho Chi Minh City behind, I lean into the window and quietly say goodbye. Mai grabs my arm and asks, "Daddy, is this where you are from?" She points to the city out the window, but before I can answer she continues, "Are you a Vietnamese?" I touch her face and look into her eyes. "I am neither Vietnamese nor Canadian," I say, and she scratches her head confusedly.

"My blood is the blood of the Vietnamese people. Vietnam is the country where I was born and grew up, where I had a mother, a father, and siblings. It is the country I came from, and it is first and foremost who I am. But Canada nurtured and cared for me when I was in need. It is a place that will forever define my life from the moment I stepped onto its soil. Canadians accepted me and turned me into a contributing member of society. I am a Vietnamese-Canadian. I carry both homelands within me, and both of these cultures define who I am. I am the luckiest of men, because I have enjoyed the luxuries of two different worlds."

Mai is delighted to have the blood and the splendor of both worlds within her. She will walk through life like two people sharing the same goals and minds.

Made in the USA
Charleston, SC
27 March 2013